I0742034

Debarim Publishing
807 W Broadway St. Spiro, OK 74959
www.debarimpublishing.com

Paperback ISBN-13: 979-8-9924767-5-0
Ebook ISBN-13: 979-8-9924767-6-7

For those who support me along each step of my journey <3

After The Coming

Book One of The Coming Series

R. Durham

Table of Contents

Chapter One

Jamal is Taken

"Miss Ray! Miss Ray! They got Jamal! Hurry, they're gonna kill 'im!" Lola may have a flair for the dramatic, but her little brother definitely has a knack for getting into trouble. With a little groan, I roll out of bed, glancing out my window to see that it is barely daybreak, and once again, I've only been asleep for a few hours. No time to worry about it now, though. I grab the nearest pair of worn-out jeans from the heap on the floor and quickly pull them on. *Maybe one of these days I'll have enough time to deal with this mess.*

Entering the living room, "Who has him, Lola?" I respond to the young woman pacing back and forth across the small space.

"It's that Lalonda's gang, they grabbed 'im up and took 'im to The Restaurant, said he stole somethin' of hers and they gonna make 'im pay! We gotta hurry quick, Miss Ray, 'fore they do somethin' awful!"

This sweet girl's southern accent always comes on so much thicker when she's in a hurry, and this is no exception.

Everyone knew The Restaurant. It was the only public eatery left in town after The Coming and the headquarters for one of the most ruthless, egotistical gang leaders I had ever met. It used to be called Leonelli's, but the new owner seemed to hate it when anyone called it that. Its generic name is the best anyone has for it.

Lalonda was a woman who had once been a real beauty, and rumor has it, a promising singer. However, years of being an evil person have a way of twisting one's features. Almost as if the inner demons want to show off the work they have done, destroying a soul by reflecting that inner turmoil on the outside. The odd part of it all is that she is still in her 20s but appears so much older. Most days, I felt sorry for her, but days like today, her actions remind me just how dangerous she can be.

Quickly walking out the front door to the driveway, Lola and I jump into my truck, despite the limited gas supply. Who knew how much time we had before Lalonda did something crazy to that poor 15-year-old boy.

I'd never had the chance to tell my dear daddy how much I appreciated the old truck. He had fully restored the dark green 1946 Ford pickup that belonged to his father and kept it safe in the old barn out at the farmhouse. Being a classic, it was one of the only vehicles that didn't go down in the attacks, and given that it was granddaddy's before it was his, I was proud to drive it from time to time. Days like this, though, the ride wasn't as enjoyable.

As we pulled up to the front of The Restaurant, I could already see through the open doors that there was quite a crowd inside, no doubt there to see the spectacle she was putting on. *Don't people have anything better to do?*

"Great, nothing like a mob to get her going," I mumble to myself as we walk to the double doors. Entering this place was never on my list of favorite things to do, but it had to be done if anyone was going to reason with this woman.

Pushing our way through the crowd, I finally see Jamal in the center of the seating area, tied down to a chair, his right arm held down on top of a table by the ever-present hulk of a man, Bruno, Lalonda's silent and formidable right-hand man.

"I know you stole my diamonds, Jamal. I will have them back and your hand, too, you little *thief*!" Lalonda, never one to let anyone else have the spotlight, was walking slowly around the table and chair where Jamal was frozen in place, both by fear and the wires tied around his other arm, legs, and waist.

"I never took nuthin' Miss Lalonda, promise!" squeaked the terrified boy, certain that this vicious woman's reputation for readily harming others would surely claim his hand, if not his life.

"Then tell me who did it if it wasn't you!" she shouted inches from Jamal's face as she slammed the butcher's knife down onto the worn veneer finish of the tabletop and leaned over it to stare into Jamal's face.

"I don' know Miss Lalonda, honest! Why would I steal from you? You crazy!" Jamal shrieks in absolute terror.

"AH HAHAHAHAHA!" The cackling of the unstable woman filled the air as Lalonda threw her head back, before stabbing the tip of the knife she has been waving around into the table just millimeters from Jamal's fingertips. "Crazy? You ain't seen nothin' yet!"

"Alright, that's enough!" I shout as Lalonda raises the blade back above her head. She stops to look at me before lowering it back down and continuing her dramatics.

"Oh great. Watch out, everyone. The bleeding heart just walked in, and she leaks!"

It must be nice to have so many people standing by to laugh at poor wit and stroke your ego. *Not a time for insults, Ray.*

"May I ask just what is going on here?" I ask as I move into the center of the room.

"Isn't it obvious? This little rat of yours has stolen some of my cheese and got caught in the trap." Sneered Lalonda. It's sad how someone who was once so outwardly beautiful could make her face contort so heavily.

"And what is it you say he's stolen?" I ask, keeping in mind my early training with animals, to always maintain a smooth, even, lower tone of voice to induce calm as you approach.

"My diamonds! My beautiful bag of diamonds. It was here when I employed this brat to run an errand for me and then *mysteriously* went missing right after he left."

The obvious sarcasm brought another chuckle from the crowd, as if Lalonda's antics amused them, as well as the subtle fear of her wrath should they not take her side.

"Do you have any proof that it was Jamal?" My arms cross subconsciously, knowing I need to be on the defensive.

"What proof do I need? I say he's guilty and I'm going to punish him as a thief!" Again, brandishing the knife to illustrate her point.

"There's no need for that just yet. Until an investigation has been done, it isn't going to help anyone, including you, to punish this boy. Release him to me, or at the very least allow me to talk to him, then give me some time to look into what happened. I will bring you the truth, even if it shows that Jamal is guilty."

I hope she will be easily swayed. I'm too tired for a full-on fight today.

"*I* don't have to do anything! Who do you think you are to come into *my* place and make demands?" she says, now pointing the knife in my direction.

I hold my hands up to shoulder height before responding. "I'm not here to make demands, I simply want to offer assistance in finding out who stole your diamonds and getting them back to you. I agree that whoever is guilty should receive a consequence, and I also want to be sure it is the right person. We all know that your relationship with a lot of the community is tenuous at best, and many avoid you, your business, and your employees because of it. Wouldn't it be helpful for business if they saw that you are a reasonable leader and someone who can be trusted to be fair? Besides, the people on The Hillside will likely be interested to know that you handled this judiciously, and as a large portion of what remains of town, this could make a difference for you in the future as well." I argue, knowing that she probably doesn't understand portions of my vocabulary, but would never want to appear ignorant in front of her followers. Besides, she has never been one to turn down the idea of a deal.

"What I am suggesting is a situation where everyone wins, well, everyone but whoever is guilty of this crime, that is. You will either get your diamonds back, or have the satisfaction of meeting out justice as you see fit, the order that comes from law, even unofficially, will have had its chance to work, and the town remains at peace."

Lalonda pauses briefly, tapping the back edge of her blade on her chin as she thinks. "I tell you what, I will give you until sundown to be back here with the diamonds and the thief, or I don't just take his hand, I take all of him to the outlands and let whatever happens, happen. Then his debt will go to you instead."

Again, that sneer crosses her face at the thought of the stories that come from those who claim to have been witnesses to atrocities on the other side of the border and the idea that she might finally have something over me. Reluctantly, I offer my right hand.

"You have a deal."

Lalonda waves my hand away as if even its presence is beneath her.

"Can I take him with me then? It will help save time, and the sooner I figure this out, the sooner you will have your answer." Her pointed finger answers loudly before her mouth can have a chance.

"Nice try, but no, the boy stays here with me. Can't have you both skipping town now, can we? Oh, wait, you wouldn't do that, you're too much of a *goodie-goodie*; he isn't, though, and you are just one woman after all. He could slip away from you, then where would we be? No, I think him staying here is the best answer, and since they are *my* diamonds, my word is final." Lalonda's sarcastic demands only bring further snickers from the audience and leaves a look of satisfaction across her face.

Naturally, things couldn't be simpler. I'm not worried about it, and the lack of faith in my integrity is a minor annoyance that is not worth further consideration.

"Ok, we can do this your way, but I do still need to speak with him."

"Fine. Bruno, take them to the supply closet. The rest of you, either order some food or leave. I have some thinking to do." Lalonda turns, headed for her favorite seat, the large round booth in the back corner.

The closet is just what you would expect: small, dirty, and surprisingly, still full of paper goods and cleaning supplies.

"Jamal, what are you doing running errands here?" I ask, motioning toward the door Bruno had roughly shoved us through.

"I wanted to work some time with 'er so I could ask for a cake for Mama Lou's birthday," he said into his hands, spirit obviously broken and crying from the weight of the situation.

I pull him close into as much of a hug as one can manage, sitting on the floor of the tiny space. I'd known this boy most of his life, and he felt as much a part of my own family as he was Mama Lou's.

"Oh, Jamal, why didn't you come to me? I could have helped you make a cake."

"You always so busy runnin' around fixin' things for people, I didn' wanna bother you," he said, finally looking at me.

He was right; I am too busy for everyday things. It's always putting out fires and solving problems, going from one crisis to the next, barely laying my head on the pillow, and it's still not enough. There is always one more project, one more person in trouble, one more need to be met. If vacations were still a thing people did, I think I would take a month off near a quiet piece of river with nothing but trees and the breeze to keep me company.

"Well, what's done is done. Tell me what happened from when you arrived to run the errand til I walked in just a bit ago." Jamal pulls away, still seated on the floor.

"One of Miss Lalonda's guys come up to the house in her pink Cadillac and says I has to go with 'im an' see Miss Lalonda 'cause she has a job for me. I got in and we came 'ere to a room in the back I never seen. Miss Lalonda says she needs me to take a letter to the Sheriff for her, then the man that brought me 'ere pushed me out the back door into the alley. I almos' run into this country man on accoun'a he pushed me so hard."

"Did you recognize the man at all? Would he have seen what you had in your hands?"

"I don't 'member ever seeing 'im afore. He might maybe 'ave seen what I had, cain't be sure though." He drops his head onto his knees, now hugged tightly to his chest, sobbing quietly.

"What am I gonna do, Miss Ray? They ain't never gonna let me go!"

I hug him closer, trying to reassure him. I remind him of 2 Timothy 1:7.

"Do you remember the words on the painting in my living room?

'For God hath not given us a spirit of fear; but of power, and of love, and of a sound mind.'

What does that say to you?

"It says God didn' make me scared, but Miss Lalonda sure did!"

I can't help but chuckle just a bit as I hug him tighter. "It means that when we trust in God, He will give us the power over our fear and the ability to think clearly through our situation. We don't have to be afraid of all the craziness in this world. There is much that God tells us in His Word about fear, and it all boils down to the truth; that He will care for us in this life and the next. Sometimes that help comes in the form of a person, so in the meantime, I need to go figure out how to get you out of this mess!"

"Miss Ray, I can draw that man for you real quick. I think 'e was from up on the mountain where the country folk be livin'.'"

He excitedly grabs a paper napkin off the shelf and a pencil someone had left on the long, discarded cleaning schedule clipboard. Almost as if the hands of a master artist replace the long, clumsy fingers of this precious boy, lines and shading appear on the page, forming a nearly perfect rendering of a man's face. I never knew he had this talent for art, especially for something as complex as faces. I hope we can explore it more after this is all over.

Chapter Two

The Man on the Napkin

It's a long ride up the mountain to the North of town. There are many winding roads that were difficult to navigate in the past, especially when they were not regularly maintained. In the time since the coming, these roads are hardly used at all, making it even harder to convince this old truck that I knew what I was doing. More than once, a hidden rock, stick, or pothole would reaffirm those fears. Daddy had done an excellent job when he fixed her up, and even though it was rough going, everything held and did precisely what it was designed to do. Had I not been so preoccupied with not crashing down the mountain, I might have allowed more than a brief thought to consider just how similar this situation is to life and God's plan for it.

After what seemed like hours compared to the 30 minutes it took for me to arrive, I pulled up to the tree trunk blockade at the end of the road, which is as close as you can get to the lower country folk on four wheels without an invitation. How I wished I'd grabbed my hiking boots this morning instead of my old sneakers before running out the door. It was too late now; these would have to do. Thankfully, I keep water in the truck in case I have to walk somewhere unexpectedly, so I grab the canteen with a long paracord strap, sling it crosswise over my body, and start my way further up the mountain. At least it's a pleasant day. The weather has been unpredictable this week, and it could be much worse than it is now.

Coming closer to the buildings, the air abruptly fills with gunshots from the upper mountain. Stopping to take cover behind one of the thick oak trees, I can see holes appear as bullets rip through one side, and out the other side of an open two-story metal building. Looking inside, there is a group of people huddled together in the center. The older adults and teenagers have positioned themselves on the side nearest the fire, so the younger kids are behind them.

Suddenly, a boy in overalls and a torn, dirty white shirt is hit. He screams out in pain, and a man known to be the leader of the lower folk appears, waving a piece of red material. Just as quickly as they started, the shots stopped. Unable to sit still any longer, I run into the building to try to help the teenage boy. A quick examination showed that the bullet went straight through the muscle of his upper right shoulder. It appeared that his lung and major blood supply were all unharmed, but with the trajectory and location of the wound, the upper portion of the scapula would be damaged. Without the ability or skills to perform surgery, he would have to heal as it was.

After taking a breath and the chance to look around, I realized that this brave boy would live, but the much younger boy he was trying to protect was already dead. Enraged at this, I jumped up, looking for the man with the fabric, remembering from long ago that his name was Jonathan.

"Jonathan! Jonathan, where did you go? Do you see what has happened here? What on Earth is going on?" I didn't mean to screech so, but my voice betrayed just how emotional this situation had made me.

"Sarah Beth had a baby. We had to keep the numbers," he said as he looked away, obviously ashamed, but resigned to the rule of their law.

"What do you mean, keep the numbers?" I ask, horrified that I already imagined the answer.

"We only have so much food and so much room. Cain't be addin' no more, so if'n nobody has died before a new baby comes, we all draw to see who stands in the barn. The upper folk shoots at the barn so nobody knows who done it, and we stop 'em when someone falls."

Looking at this pudgy, middle-aged mountain man in nothing but tattered overalls and a broken straw hat, I realized he didn't know any better than what he just saw. Life was hard all around, and lots of strange ideas come out of a shocking life change, such as we have all experienced. Some ideas are so much worse than others, though. The sadness of it all threatened to overwhelm the collected façade I try so hard to maintain. I had to get back to business if I was to have any hope of saving the other boy hanging in the balance today.

Pulling out the napkin, I showed it to Jonathan. "Do you know this man? He may have witnessed something yesterday down in town that could make a huge difference for another young boy's life." Looking at the lifeless body of the child being carried away for burial preparations.

"The boy is being accused of a crime, I don't believe he committed, and I am here hoping you can help me find this man so I might find evidence to exonerate him." Jonathan scratches his scruffy chin as he looks at the drawing.

"Yeah, I know that guy. That's my nephew Joshua Pierce. He has a place out a ways up the mountain. He keeps to hisself, though, none of us see him much, and I don't know for sure that he's there. We'll have to go through Cooper's land to get there, so we best talk to him first."

Before I can thank him for his help, he turns and walks off at a surprisingly brisk pace. I almost have to jog to keep up with him, but it's worth it if it means saving time. As we go through the buildings of the lower folk, I see curious young faces peeking out from open doors and windows and under porches. Not a clean face in the bunch, and most of the clothes that are worn are tattered and filthy to match. Many of the buildings are old mobile home trailers with broken windows and missing tin siding. One even has an old blue tarp and wooden pallets for a roof. The poverty of it all is heartbreaking and nags at my soul. These people need help too, but are they even willing to help themselves?

A few minutes later, Jonathan is shouting at the front of what was once a beautiful white ranch house. The wood shows its age and the lack of care it once knew. The yard likewise has long been neglected. It seems both sides of the country community have seen a long, rough spell.

"Cooper! You in there? Come out and see me!"

"Quit yer hollerin', you old fool! I ain't deaf and I ain't got nothin' to say to you anyhow!"

The shout comes from the side of the house. As we walk around, a small dilapidated porch is struggling to hold up an older man, much shorter and thinner than Jonathan, but also wearing only overalls and a hat long overdue for a trip to the burn heap.

"Now Cooper, what's got yer dander all up today?"

"You do! You need to get better control of yer women so I don't have to keep wasting bullets fixing yer mouth problems! Do you think I like the idea of killin' kin?"

His rocking chair is loudly squeaking its complaints from the strain as he pumps it back and forth with considerable force. I instantly appreciated the dynamic between these two and the realization that this ritual was not taken as lightly as was first thought.

"I cain't help it if young'uns run off together cause they're *in looove* and do some fool thing like getting theyselves pregnant. I didn't do it, ya know!"

Jonathan says, firmly crossing his arms, and obviously still feeling shame despite his defense.

Cooper sighs and lowers his voice. "I know you didn't, Johnny, I just can't reckon over how wrong this thing is. I wish there was another way."

Looking into his lap, Cooper's shame is just as apparent, and I can't help but feel a deepening desire to help this community. I will have to come back up here when things calm down in town. I think I may have a few ideas looking at this place that could change things for the better.

"So, who did you bring with ya? Are you gonna introduce us or what?"

Standing up out of his chair, Cooper offers his right hand in my direction.

"My name is Ray Weber, Sir. It is very nice to meet you." I return a firm handshake just as Daddy taught me.

"Ray, huh? Didn't yer daddy know you was a girl?"

Releasing my hand and rubbing his dramatically as if I had squeezed much too hard.

I can't help but laugh. "Of course, he knew I was a girl. Ray is short for Raylene, my Grandmama's middle name."

"Good grip though, seems he done something right with you." Sending a wink my way.

"My name is Leonard Cooper, but everyone calls me Cooper or sometimes Coop. What brings you all the way up here?"

"I'm trying to find a man who may be able to help me fix a problem down in town." I hand him the napkin drawing and continue.

"Jonathan says we need to go through your land to get to his place, so I would like to ask your permission to head that way."

"You can go, but you may not find him. He doesn't much like to be found. He was always strange, even as a young'un. That's why he keeps to hisself up the way there." He motioned with his gaze up past his house beyond the trees.

"I thank ye for asking, yer always welcome up on my portion, Miss Raylene." Another wink punctuates his playful statement. It feels nice to be recognized and respected by this simple man.

Jonathan starts walking along the tiny path past Cooper's house. It is strange to think that anyone would live up past the wild, unkempt trees and brush. As I am appreciating the calm beauty of the trees around me, suddenly Jonathan drops down and pulls me with him right before a bullet ricochets off the bark of the tree behind us.

"That dern fool's gonna kill somebody one of these days!" He spits out through clenched teeth.

"Come out slow so I can see you, I won't miss again." A man's voice commands calmly, yet firmly.

We stand with our hands visible. Jonathan shouts at the man,

"Joshua, you take another pot shot at me and it'll be yer last, I swear it on your sweet mama!"

"Don't swear on people, Uncle Jonathan, it's impolite!"

Surprised that his speech reflects a higher level of education, I found my hands lowering as my curiosity about this strange man piqued all the more.

Just starting to peek out from behind the edge of the bush we are using for cover, I still can't see Joshua.

"My name is Ray Weber. I came up the mountain to speak with you. May we come up?" I shout, hoping to sound more confident than I feel.

"Yeah, come on then," echoes down from the house hiding behind more trees.

A screen door slams shut, and as we come through the dense bushes and trees, a quaint, simple house in decent repair comes into view. Adding to the surprises of the day, the area is well kept with a small garden off to the side, a hand pump well on the corner, and a neat porch with a very comfortable-looking two-person swing seat hanging from the rafters.

"You like what you see?" says a voice, cutting through my concentrated observations.

"Oh, yes, it's beautiful! I've never seen such a well-kept place up this way. Do you live here alone?"

"Didn't you say you needed to speak with me?" He asks, deftly changing the subject as he steps back inside through a screen door. I move to follow, but decide to wait for an invitation to enter.

"Yes, sorry. Were you down in town last night near The Restaurant on Main Street? A boy is in trouble, and he thought you might have seen some things that can help clear him. He drew this picture, which is what led me to you," I say, pulling out the napkin.

"Why don't you come inside? I'll bring her back down, Uncle Jonathan. I'm sure you have matters to tend to."

Joshua looks past me at Jonathan, giving him a pointed look. It's nice to know someone else disapproves of the events of the day. Perhaps this man and I have more in common than I thought.

"I'm sorry about the poor greeting just now. I refuse to participate in their barbarisms, and almost every time that one happens, someone comes up here to give me trouble for not being part of it all. I've taken to making it so it's not worth it for them to bother. I assure you, I have excellent aim, and you weren't actually in danger. Can I get you some water and try to make it up to you a bit?" He asks, heading towards the kitchen.

"Water would be great, thank you, and thank you for the apology. It has been a rather jarring day for sure."

The inside of his house is also neat and decently well-kept. The only things out of place are the stacks of books covering every flat surface and a large portion of the floor. Looking closer, I recognize many of the books as ones I had donated to help build a library. They had gone missing from the drop-off location before they could be taken into the little alley room off of my family's store. Many people were upset at the loss, as every book was donated from local families at my request.

"Say, where did you find these books? There are so many," I say, coyly trying to see if this was a mistake, or a theft.

"You wouldn't believe me if I told you."

"Try me," I say as I walk towards the kitchen.

He comes back into the living room, hands me a tall glass of the cool drink, and continues to pick up one of the books, incidentally, one of my old favorites.

"I found them down in town one night, just tossed out in an alleyway like garbage! I don't know who would just discard so many great books, especially now when knowledge is so much harder to come by. It took me two trips to collect them all, but not a one was left to ruin.

I hope to find a way to get them out to people who are interested, especially kids. Most of the kids up here are unable to read. The adults don't care to have them learn. It is really hard to watch, so I try to stay away a lot, but help where I can."

He moves some books gently to the side to uncover two well-loved chairs.

"Would you care to sit down?" He asks, motioning to one of them.

"Yes, thank you." I sit down, relieving my tired legs, which feels much better than I expected it to.

"I go down to town from time to time to scavenge for things like clothes and such that have been tossed out. You would not believe how wasteful people still are these days. I go to the dump some also. I found a dresser last week that just needed minor repairs. It's over there waiting its turn.

There is a sweet little girl down in the lower village who comes up every so often with her brother to trade, helping in the garden for some fresh produce. I don't really need the help, but I hope they will tell their friends and maybe more of them will come up. They need the food, but I can't convince any of them to clear a section to garden. I save all of the seeds, so there is plenty to go around." He sighs, leaning back in his chair, somewhat deflated by the thought.

"It sounds like you care very deeply for people," I say, honestly impressed by his efforts. Picking up my favorite book and opening to read the inscription on the inner cover.

"I'd like to help as well once I have a little time. There are a lot of issues I'm trying to juggle down in town, including the *mysterious* disappearance of the books donated for the new library I was working on." I look up with a slight grin as I look his way. My statement had the desired effect as he appeared shocked with the realization that he had been the one to take the books, that they did have a purpose.

"To my dearest daughter, may your life be full of new adventures and the wisdom to let The Father guide your way through them. Love, Daddy." I couldn't help but hug the book of stories as I closed it like I had done so many times before.

"I'm so sorry! I had no idea they were there on purpose. I'll bring them right back down as soon as I can."

"I'd appreciate that very much, the people they came from were less than pleased with me when they went missing," I say, sending him a bigger grin.

"I've been working on getting people to focus more on the community than they do on themselves. It took a lot of talking to convince people this was a worthwhile venture, but I hope it will open the door to more community cooperation throughout town, not just the section I help to care for. Plus, I want to help keep pieces of how life was before alive. Things like art, creativity, imagination, literature," I say as I wave the book and return it to the pile next to me.

"People should remember that there was once a world of beauty that was so much more than just surviving the day-to-day. Maybe one day we will make it back to where we were, or maybe grow to be even better."

"I'm glad you have knowledge; knowledge makes such a huge difference. Look at me, I would not trade fitting in around here for the ability to create abstract thoughts and improve my circumstances." His nod towards the window and further towards the barn down the mountain is unmistakable.

Leaning forward, I place my elbows on my knees. "I'm really glad to hear that. I don't have the time or the fuel to come up here all the time to do things myself, but I had a few ideas walking through that might help things to change a bit. I was thinking about stopping to talk with Cooper and Jonathan on the way back down, if I have any time, at least to maybe set up a meeting for when I hopefully will. If you would be willing, I would love to run through some thoughts with you instead."

Joshua mirrors my actions, also leaning forward into the conversation. "I would like that very much. From what I saw, you have already earned a bit of respect around here. Those two old badgers don't listen to hardly anyone, especially townies. Maybe I can set up a time for you to come and address everyone. Things could really change around here if people were motivated to do something different."

"That sounds like a plan! Meanwhile, I still have today's emergency to work out. Would you be willing to come down with me to speak on Jamal's behalf?"

"That's right, the boy you mentioned. Where did he say he saw me?"

"He said he was being pushed out into the alleyway next to The Restaurant and about ran you over. We were hoping you might have noticed whether he was holding anything, specifically a small bag. Supposedly, he stole it from Lalonda, and she is literally out for blood. I'm supposed to find the bag and the thief by sundown or things will not go well for the boy, or for me."

"I remember that, yes. I was coming up the alley, and a teenage boy was pushed right into me. In all fairness, there was a dumpster right there, so they probably didn't see me. I didn't see anything with the boy, and I try not to be seen going into any of the dumpsters in case someone might not appreciate my efforts, so I moved to the side away from the door.

The man who had pushed him stayed outside to smoke a cigarette. He hid something behind the dumpster in a hole in the wall and seemed to be waiting for someone. A few minutes later, I saw a man in what looked like a deputy uniform come and speak with him. They talked briefly, and the deputy seemed agitated, but the bag never came out. I couldn't hear everything, but it sounded like Lalonda's man said that the deputy would be paid when 'it is done'. He was called back inside, and the deputy left quickly. I didn't want to get caught, so I left.

I wasn't doing anything wrong, but a lot of people see my clothes and assume I'm doing something I shouldn't be. In reality, all I was doing was checking the dumpsters to see if there was anything usable in the trash. Real glamorous, huh?"

"Not glamorous, but understandable. I think we have been crossing paths without knowing it. I take a group around every so often, working our way through burned buildings and abandoned places, taking useful items, canned goods, and such to add to a store of sorts. People don't have to pay money, but we ration and try to find ways to trade work for the goods.

That may seem odd given that we only collected the items, but it is a good way to make people feel useful and regain some pride in having earned something. We have also been building a list of who has what skills so we can best distribute the work that needs done. So far, it has been an excellent program. We have done little trash checks, but I just started up a plan to start sorting trash out to compost, reusables, firewood, etc., to hopefully be done in an empty warehouse we found near the center of town.

Eventually, we will be able to collect usable building materials as the burnt buildings are taken down to possibly start building new places and repairing others that just need a little bit to be usable again."

"Wow!" Joshua leans back into his chair. "You weren't kidding when you mentioned you have some ideas to improve things! I am seriously impressed!" I smile just a bit, but then return to being serious and turn the conversation back to Jamal.

"Ideas are great, but if I don't figure out this theft issue, I may not be around to do much with them. Would you mind talking more as we head down? I think you may know where the bag is, and if so, we just might be able to talk her down."

"I'm ready if you are."

Chapter Three

A Deal is a Deal

Pulling into town, I let Joshua out of the truck a building away from The Restaurant so he can go around to the side of the building while I enter through the front. *Hopefully, whatever had been hidden is still there.* Without waiting to see what Joshua found, I head inside to make sure Jamal is still there and unharmed.

"She's been expecting you," came a snide comment from one of Lalonda's men at the door.

"Well, let's not disappoint her, then, shall we?"

The restaurant seems even fuller than it was this morning, no doubt in anticipation of the conversation we are about to have. Lalonda, Jamal, and the Sheriff are all sitting in her favorite corner booth, watching as I make my way through the crowd toward them.

"Well, if it isn't the bleeding heart come to rescue her little rat." Snickers echo around the room from what is left of the earlier crowd. If there is anything this woman loves more than herself, it is other people watching her.

"Well, I would like to discuss it."

"Where are my diamonds? And where is the thief then? Did we not have a deal?"

"The diamonds are on their way, and as for the thief, perhaps we should discuss this with a bit more privacy."

"Privacy? What would I want privacy for? I want everyone to see you fail, *the pretty princess, always saving everyone.* How lovely it will be to knock that tiara off your head for good!" The sarcastic, mocking tones she uses, meant to tear me down, only reveal just how insecure she is herself.

"I'm sorry to hear that this is how you see me. I suppose I expected a strong woman such as yourself would recognize that similarity in another person, when present. I apologize if I have offended you."

Scoffing in retort, "Of course I recognize strength, I simply don't like you."

"Fair enough, shall we discuss what I found out today?"

"Sure, let's hear all about your failure."

It is pretty difficult not to roll your eyes in the presence of someone so completely ridiculous, but years of providing customer service in my family's store taught me restraint against such things. Who knew the job my father gave me would prove so useful even now?

"In talking with Jamal before I left, he told me of one of your men shoving him out into the alleyway after your conversation soliciting his services for an errand. Jamal, can you point out the man? I'd like to make sure he doesn't leave until this is finished." Jamal stood up and quickly pointed to a man who had slowly been trying to slip out the back.

"There, the one tryin' to walk away."

"Stop him, boys, it seems we need to have a little *chat*." Lalonda is quick to respond.

Two of her other men grab him and bring him back towards the booth.

"Let go of me, I didn't do nothin'!" the man screeches through clenched teeth.

"Brady? You better not have been betraying me. You remember the last one who did that, right?"

"But I didn't do nothin'! You gonna believe this *princess* over me?" Nearly begging, Brady is pushed down hard into a chair.

"Ok, you got him here, get to it already. I'm hungry for some justice!" Rubbing her hands together as if preparing for a good meal.

"Jamal told me that he nearly crashed into a man who was walking through the alley after he was shoved out the back door, and he was able to draw me this picture." I lay the napkin down on the table before her, which she immediately picks up and studies.

"I went in search of him and found him up on the mountain. He had a very interesting story to tell. Would you like me to retell it for you, or would you like to wait for him instead?"

"I can tell her if y'all will let me through here." Joshua moves through the crowd towards the booth, carrying a small black velvet bag.

"My diamonds! YOU had them!" Lalonda screeches as she lunges for the bag.

"Grab him too!" She pours the diamonds out all over the floor, and down on her knees and elbows, starts counting them, almost as if they held a spell over her.

"Ma'am, if I may, I was walking in the alleyway yesterday, just cutting through on my trip, and as I came around the dumpster, that boy there was being shoved out of the door to your kitchen. Unsure of what was happening, I backed up a ways to the other side so I could assess the situation. The man you have there in that chair is the one who shoved him out.

The boy ran off, then I observed this man smoke a cigarette and take the bag you have there out of his pocket. He hid it in a hole in the wall behind the dumpster before another man showed up. I was still unsure of what was happening and didn't want a run-in if I could help it, so I remained behind the dumpster and was able to hear part of the conversation. Your man there in the chair met with someone wearing a deputy's uniform, presumably requesting payment for a job. Your man told him he would not get paid until 'it was done'.

Now I don't know what it was that he was referring to, or I would tell you that as well. As soon as they parted, I left and went back up the mountain until Miss Ray came and found me earlier today. I just went back there and retrieved this bag for you as payment to release the boy."

"Forty-four, forty-five... Wait, what? Oh yeah, he can go. Bruno, put Brady in the freezer. I'll deal with him later. It's almost a shame, princess, I was hoping you would come back to fall on your face. There's always another day, I suppose."

She scooped up the diamonds and put them all back into the small cloth bag, which immediately went down her shirt, presumably for safekeeping.

Turning back towards me with a thoughtful grin, "Wait a minute! You know, I just realized it's just after sundown. You didn't quite keep your word. There is still a debt to be paid."

"Lalonda, you have your diamonds and the thief, what else would you require?"

"The boy belongs to me. He will do whatever I say, no matter what, or when I say it."

I should have known she would try to do something like this. "Perhaps we can find a compromise. I have recently discovered where the missing library books went off to, and have arranged for them to be returned very soon.

What if I make Jamal the librarian? He will be serving the community and being useful, which will help keep him out of trouble and out of your hair.”

“No, Miss Ray, I can’t be no librarian, whatchu thinkin’?” Jamal's fear is obvious, though masked by anger.

“No, he belongs to me. Instead of putting them in the back room of *your* store, we put them in the front room here where I can keep an eye on him.”

“Ok, then, since it would be helping you, Jamal gets to eat here.”

“Only one meal a day, no more!”

“Fair enough, he will take lunch here, a meal of his choosing, though, and he gets a minimum of two bathroom breaks.”

“Sure, then he can run my errands on his breaks.”

“No, he is the librarian; his duties are solely that of taking care of the library. He can’t do that if he is off running errands, then can he?”

“Fine, but he lives here then.”

“The library is a 9-5 job, he will be going home in the evenings and returning each day for work. Of course, all of this would have to mean that at least the front of the building is a community safe zone, otherwise this won’t work for everyone who might like to borrow a book.”

“Ugh, you’re such a pain! Fine! Now get out, I have things to do.” Her right hand clutching the fabric over the diamond’s new stronghold as she sits leaning into the Sheriff's chest.

“Thank you, Lalonda, we’ll see you in the morning, two days from now, when the books arrive.”

Finally stepping outside together, I turn to talk to Joshua, but he beats me to conversation.

“It’s late to head back up the mountain on foot, and I won’t ask you to drive that road in the dark. I have a place I keep down here anyway, so I’ll be good. I’ll see you soon with the books.” He heads off down the alleyway before I can thank him. I almost can’t believe how helpful and interesting he has been to meet. Who would have ever expected such a person to live up on the mountain? *I hope I will see him again.*

Jamal and I climb up into the truck to head home.

"Why did you do that? I ain't gonna work for that crazy lady! You had no right to do that, Miss Ray, no right!"

"Jamal, I know this doesn't look too good, but I have a plan. You, being the librarian there, gives you the opportunity to read and learn. Think about it, all day, every day, you will have the collective written knowledge of the community at your fingertips! You will even be fed a decent meal for lunch every day, saving Mama Lou from feeding you, and if you manage it well, you can probably find a way to bring something home with you.

Think of how much that will help out around the house! Now, Lalonda can't touch you because you will have a contract with the community, and she would have to answer to everyone officially if she tried to take you down again. Plus, this opens up The Restaurant to others who have been in need of the ability to find work and food for a long time. If you so choose, you can also keep an ear out for any crazy ideas coming out of that place and warn people before things happen. Jamal, you just became a massive part of making our town safer and more livable!"

I shut off the truck in front of my house, and we get out, heading up the street two houses to Mama Lou's.

"Do you see why I did this now?"

"Yeah, but I still don' like it. I'll do it, though. I hope you right 'bout this bein' good, cause it don' feel good."

"I know it doesn't, and for that I'm sorry, but I do think it will work out."

Walking up to the porch, the front door flies open wildly to reveal a very relieved Lola.

"Mama, he's home! Miss Ray has him home!"

The outline of a much stouter woman comes quickly to the door, pushing through it without pause. "Lawd have mercy. Thank ya, Jesus! Come up here and hug yo' mama, boy!" Jamal does as he is bid, more eagerly than I think he would have liked to let on.

"Let me see ya, boy." Mama Lou took Jamal's face in her hands, tears making their way down her plump ebony cheeks.

"Auntie Ray!" Matthew cries, having followed Mama Lou to see what the commotion was about.

"Hey buddy, I missed you today! Did you have fun with Miss Lola?"

"Yeah! We played in the back yard with the dirt and made stick people, then made mud pies."

"I see the mud part for sure!"

It felt good to laugh a bit after such a rough day.

"Thank you, Lola, Mama Lou. We'll head home now. Jamal has a job as the new librarian starting the day after tomorrow. I'm going to help him get it set up, but he can tell you all about it."

"Thank you again, Ray, I don' know what I'd do without ma boy or without a frien' like you."

Gently cradling her upper arm with my hand, I reply, "Mama Lou, I don't know what I'd do without you either!"

Chapter Four

What Do You Expect?

Looking at the clock when Matthew and I make it home, it's hard to believe that it's only 7:30, unless of course I forgot to wind the thing again. It's a beautiful, oak grandfather clock that my mama's daddy had left to my brother when he passed, along with this house and everything else in it.

The clock was handmade in Switzerland, supposedly in the early 1900's and had been in the family for five generations now, if you include Matthew. Thankfully, it was also entirely mechanical, so I had a working clock in the main room.

Going to the kitchen, I remember that I haven't really eaten again today. That seems to be a trend lately, and one I really should be better about changing. Thankfully, the garden is doing well, and we have some fresh tomatoes ready to pick.

I set Matthew up at the sink, scrubbing off some of the dirt from the day. It takes a lot of water to fill the tub and hand pumping it from the well then heating it on the wood stove is just not something I'm willing to do right now.

The lantern I use gives just enough light that I can see which tomatoes are ripe or not. The backyard is small, typical of the houses here in town and open enough that I can also usually get a decent idea if there are any creatures out back that shouldn't be from the back porch. With the electricity out, there is a lot less light and noise to keep animals away, so it's pretty common to find a visitor or two when you go out at night.

Dinner will be simple tonight: tomato sandwiches. I so wish we had avocados right now and some turkey bacon. I really need to stop thinking about foods like that, but sometimes it's nice to remember a time before all of this. Preparing the simple meal takes only a couple of minutes. Thankfully, Matthew isn't very picky, and he loves tomatoes.

"Matthew, are you all cleaned up? I have a tomato sandwich for you." I call down the hallway to the bathroom where he is getting washed up.

I can hear his pace quicken as he finishes dressing in his pajamas. "Yes ma'am!"

What did I do to deserve such a great kid? I know he wasn't born to me, but I love him as if he was. He's so young, but so in tune with what is going on around him, yet very optimistic and upbeat in spite of it all. If I had to pick a hero, it just might be him.

"That looks yummy, Auntie Ray, thank you."

Matthew quickly climbs up one of the two bar-height stools in the small kitchen.

"I'm really hungry after playing all day. There were more kids today, and it was fun, but Kevin wasn't very nice. I don't think he is very happy."

"Is Kevin new?" I ask, unfamiliar with a child with that name.

"Yeah, I don't think he has parents, like me, but I'm not sure he has an auntie either."

"That's too bad. Maybe he will keep coming so you can make friends with him."

"I hope so, I would like to help him be happy."

"You're such a sweet boy, Matthew. I love you very much."

"I love you, too, Auntie Ray."

"Let's pray. Our precious and heavenly Father, we thank you for another day with a roof over our heads, clothes on our backs, and food for our stomachs. We thank you for the safety and the love in this house, Father. We ask that you keep your hand over this town, its people, and the disappeared ones. We also want to tell you about Kevin today, Father. It looks like he is alone and could really use some help. Teach us what to say and do to be your hands and feet for him. We thank you and praise you. It's in Yeshua's name we pray, Amen."

"Amen," echoes Matthew.

It's 8:30, Matthew is in bed, and I still have several inches of crocheting to do before tomorrow. Just as I am settling into the chair, I hear a knock at the door.

"Just a minute," I call out.

I'm really not interested in any more issues today, I just want to finish this project so I can keep my word. I open the door and, to my surprise, find Joshua standing there.

"Oh, hello! I thought you said you had somewhere you were going."

"Oh, I do have somewhere to stay, I just thought perhaps we could talk some more about some of your ideas. I'd love to have more to discuss with Cooper and Uncle Jonathan when I go back up tomorrow."

"I'm sorry, yes, please come in. I apologize for my rudeness. I think I'm ready for bed already." A strangely nervous chuckle follows. *Why am I nervous?*

"Please, have a seat. Can I get you some water?"

"Water sounds great, thank you," Joshua replies as he settles onto the antique love seat just inside the front door.

"You have a lovely home." He calls into the kitchen.

Surprisingly, I had a couple of clean glasses left.

"Thank you. It's actually my brother's place. I didn't feel like staying out at my family's farm was a good idea after everything, and Matthew has lost enough without having to leave his home, too."

Handing him the glass of water, I sit back in the high-backed antique chair my sister-in-law, Ginny, had bought when they moved into this house, and pick the crochet mat back up.

"Matthew?"

"Yes, my nephew. He's five and one of the most amazing kids. My sister-in-law passed away when he was born, and my brother was a soldier at the fort south of town. I think he disappeared during The Coming, and my parents too. So it's just me and Matthew."

"Oh wow, I'm so sorry to hear that. With so many similar stories out there, it's a blessing you are still here for Matthew." Joshua's genuine concern and thoughtfulness are another pleasant surprise, and yet feel so familiar somehow.

"That's an interesting project you have there." Gesturing to the mat I'm now working on again.

"Yes, it is a sleeping mat. I, and a few other ladies on the hillside make the mats for some of the homeless kids. It isn't a mattress, but it is better than nothing. I have been employing kids around the neighborhood to collect plastic shopping bags for me, rewarding them with food or the occasional sweets in trade for them. It gives them something to do, the pride of earning something, and it keeps me stocked with plastic bags, which I use to make the plarn to crochet.

The Embry twins were supposed to come by tomorrow for the mats I promised them, and I still have this one to finish."

"Wow, that's actually really creative. You've implemented some really great ideas down here; I'll keep an eye out for any useful bags while I'm out. I hope we can find some new ideas to try on the mountain, and that those old codgers will listen to them!"

"I'd really appreciate it. They haven't been coming in as fast anymore, and I'm a little afraid we will run out before enough have been made.

I'd really like to find a way to get the school or something going again. I've been thinking that maybe we can turn the gym into a dorm so the homeless kids have a safe place to sleep and eventually start some classes up again. The kids would get into far less trouble with a little more supervision and purpose.

I'm having trouble with community backing, though. One battle at a time, I suppose."

A heavier sigh than I intended shows my frustration. "People are quick to find ways to help themselves, but haven't been as supportive in other ways. It's understandable, but I hope for better. I don't mean to sound so down about it, but the truth is that some days the reality of life now gets to me more than others. I just get tired trying to keep things going, you know?"

"I don't blame you even a little. You are doing so much for the community here. I almost can't even see how one person could manage so much. You really are amazing!"

"You better be careful or I just might believe you!" A small grin is finding its way into my cheeks when suddenly someone is pounding on the door. Both of us jump up, but before I can get to the door, Joshua has it open.

"Miss Ray! Miss Ray! They got 'im and hurt 'im real bad!"

Lola and Mama Lou have Jamal propped up between them. From what I can see, he has been badly beaten. Joshua reaches in to take over carrying him.

"Take him down the hall to the last room on the left and get his outer clothes off. I'll be right there."

While Joshua and the ladies get Jamal moved through the house, I run out to the herb side of the garden and pick a healthy handful of comfrey, arnica, marjoram, and some lavender. I'll have to go back out to find some birch later. *Knew I should have restocked the birch.*

I don't know what I would do without my grandma's herb garden when things like this come up. Going back inside, Mama Lou is beside herself, upset.

"Look what they done to ma boy, Miss Ray! They'd killed 'im dead if'n I didn' see them! Why would they do this to my sweet boy?" Sobs have taken over as the only sound she has left.

I lay a hand on her shoulder, "Mama Lou, I know you're worried, but can you help me? I need you to go pump some water into the clean water bucket and start some water to boil, please. Then bring some clean water in a bowl in here."

Lola and Joshua have taken his clothes off down to his boxers, revealing quite a bit of blood and many bruises already coming up. Most of the blows look to have been to his face and torso.

I try to carefully check his abdomen for any internal bleeding, but do not see any signs until he begins to cough and expels a bit of blood. Hopefully, it is just a bruised lung. Grabbing the stethoscope from the table next to the bed, I listen to different areas of his chest. His heart and lungs sound normal, and considering the abuse they have just taken, that is a huge relief. Most importantly, his lungs sound clear, and both are filling the way they should.

"How can I help?" Joshua asks from beside me.

"I need you to help me make a paste out of these herbs. Do you know how to use that?" I point to the large mortar and pestle on the antique roll top desk I use as an apothecary.

"Yes, I can do that." Joshua takes the tools and herbs I brought in from the garden and begins to strip and crush them. *It's nice to have help around on a day like this.*

"Do you know what happened? Who did this?" I ask.

Lola speaks up on behalf of everyone, "It was Miss Lalonda's men. They said they's gonna make 'im break 'is word and not show up to work so she could do whatever she wanted with 'im."

I close my eyes and shake my head, "Oh, Jamal, I'm so sorry. This never should have happened. I will take you to The Restaurant myself and we will keep our word, whether she likes it or not."

I wish I were surprised by this turn of events, but little about the evil that woman spreads is surprising anymore. It doesn't stop the anger stirred from the hurt of knowing I had a part in the pain Jamal is in right now, and that I wasn't there to stop it when it happened.

Mama Lou brings in the water in a bowl, and I carefully clean off the blood from his face and body. It reveals more bruises and a few small scrapes. It could definitely have been worse, but it was bad enough regardless.

"Is this about the consistency you want?" Joshua shows me the paste he has made.

"This looks really good, actually, thank you."

Returning my attention towards the bed, "Now Jamal, this is not going to feel very good at first, but once I wrap it up, it should relieve some of the pain.

Lola, can you grab a sheet out of the hall closet?

Joshua, I'm going to need you to help him up just enough that I can slide this fabric underneath him. Jamal, I know this is going to hurt, we are going to be as careful as we can be, ok?"

I cut a long strip of fabric from the sheet that is approximately as wide as Jamal's back is long. Then we coat the portion of the sheet that will sit underneath his back with the paste. Joshua is actually very gentle lifting Jamal up as Lola and I slide the sheet underneath him.

"You're doing so well, Jamal, great job! I'm just going to put some more of this paste on the front, then we'll move one more time and be done, ok?"

The paste is cool, and his temperature is beginning to lower. His system has suffered so much stress that temperature control is lower on its to-do list, and his temperature dropping is causing him to shiver, which naturally hurts, given his condition. I was hoping we would avoid that, but it is happening faster than I had expected. Once we have him wrapped up, it will be better, and we can get blankets over him as well.

As Joshua and I finish wrapping him, Lola grabs a couple more pillows from the closet to help keep him propped up a bit. She has helped me enough times, she knows where a lot of things are, and how I tend to use them. I hope one day she will pick up a bit more and begin to help heal people as well.

Mama Lou brings in the tea kettle and sets it on a trivet on the herb table.

"What you want to put in this, Ray?"

"We need to add some of the dry herbs labeled *Healing Blend* from the jar on the shelf. There should be mugs and a tea ball in the kitchen cabinet next to the sink. I want to see if we can't get him to drink a bit of the tea to help bring his temperature up, also."

"I'll get it, Miss Ray," Lola says, then she is gone and back quickly, which is good. The sooner these herbs can get to work, the sooner Jamal will be on the mend.

"Stay with him, Lola, help him sip some of the tea. Hold it near him so he can smell the steam between sips. I'll be out in the living room if you need me."

"Yes, ma'am." Lola solemnly responds.

I reach up and gently squeeze her shoulder.

"He's going to be ok, Lola."

She sniffles and nods, trying to keep the emotions from spilling out, admirably strong for her 17 years.

Joshua and I go to wash off the remnants left from caring for Jamal in the kitchen sink bucket. Returning to the living room, it feels good to sit after all of today's events. Joshua sits down as well, and I notice that I'm comfortable in his presence, which is unusual considering that we only met this morning.

"Some day, huh?" Joshua asks, trying to break through the stillness in the air.

"You're telling me! I'm ready for this day to be over, I think. I wish I could say life wasn't always like this, but I'm beginning to feel like this is just the new normal. It's rare to just be able to rest or find peace anymore. I find I miss a lot of things from before."

Realizing I still haven't finished the sleeping mat, I start to crochet again.

Joshua is back on the love seat and crosses his legs with his right ankle up on his left knee.

"What sort of things?"

"Oh gosh! Running water for starters!" Laughing is a much-needed relief after a tense day like today.

"Trips out to the pond in the back pasture to fish early in the morning when it's quiet and cool, time to sit and lose myself in a good book up in the hayloft of the barn... Anyway, missing things isn't helpful when things need to be done, though, is it?"

I can't help but feel sad again, thinking of the people I miss and those moments I didn't mention. Given that I've never been able to really hide my feelings, I'm sure it's noticeable.

Joshua's empathetic tone interrupts my thoughts. "Those all sound like great things to miss. Some of them are still quite doable, though. Perhaps there is a way to have a bit of that back."

"Oh, it's ok. The freedoms of a child, I suppose. What about you?" I shrug off the sadness, changing the subject.

"Hmm, well, life hasn't really changed too much for me. I had already gone back up on the mountain before it all happened. I do wish things could go back to the way they were before, when several of the men had jobs down here to help with things like groceries. The numbers lottery wasn't always a thing; several of the elders decided on it after it was obvious that food was going to be a problem. Myself and a few others tried to talk them out of it, but so many of the men who were no longer providing were happy to go along with it and were the first to go into the barn. Very dark days."

"That's terrible! Yet another part of this already tragic period to dislike. Hopefully, we can work out some things to improve life up there so they will see that this isn't necessary." My stubborn resolve furrowing my brow at the thought.

Joshua agrees, "I hope so too. There are too few people fighting for good, it seems. This world definitely needs more of that."

Chapter Five

Soldiers

After a long night of tending to Jamal, I am finally getting to a few chores in the early hours before things will have a chance to be busy again. Joshua left around 11 pm last night, and I was too tired to stay up and finish the last mat. I hate the idea that I would not have kept my word, especially to kids who already have such a hard go of it. Hopefully, I can finish it before they arrive today.

The unexpected sound of large diesel engines breaks through the quiet of the morning. It's easy to tell that more than one vehicle has come down the street and stopped in front of the house. Moments later, there is yet another person pounding on my door, only this time, I don't know who it is.

"Hello? Open up, I need to speak with you."

"Who is it?"

"My name is Captain Stanford, ma'am. May I come in, please?"

"Yes, that's fine."

The door opens to reveal a tall man in a multicam print OCP uniform. His rank indeed reflects that of a Captain, but I can't help but notice something seems off about him.

"Hi, I'm looking for Ray Weber."

"Yes, may I ask what this is about?"

"You're Ray?"

"Yeesss." I draw out, too tired and short of patience for this conversation.

"I was told down the road that I needed to come speak with you. It seems you are the... ahh... person in charge around here." His doubtful gaze looking at the strange project in my hands.

I can't help but chuckle.

"There isn't really a formal governing body or hierarchy around here, really, just people. It just happens that I have a bit more common sense than most, so they listen when I have something to say."

"I see. Well, I come to you in search of assistance with your townsfolk."

A tinge of annoyance laces his voice, no doubt due to his surprise since he was obviously prepared to speak with a man, and because of my continued work on the mat in my hands, which is taking up a portion of my direct attention.

The Captain continues, "The government is beginning to reform and is sending out scouting missions such as ours to see who is left and where aid is most needed as they begin to re-establish control of our great nation. To help with this mission, we stop at every town we come to and ask for recruits and any extra supplies available to feed them while they are trained and added to our numbers. A counterattack is currently being designed and hopefully will be quickly executed. Most importantly, we are making sure that order is restored and that our efforts will be supported by the local populace."

I respond without looking up, still focused on my task. "Well, that makes sense, you definitely won't get far if people view you as a threat. Speaking of, you may want to shut those things off. People are not likely to be too fond of all that noise. We've gotten used to things being a bit quieter anymore."

The frustration coming from the Captain is almost palpable at this point. He probably hasn't dealt with anyone like me before. Given that the nearest military post is just a few miles south of us, we may have been his first stop.

"Ma'am, I must admit, I find your attitude and lack of respect for me a bit aggravating. I believe my position demands such respect, and the least you could do is stop fiddling with that mess and look at me when I'm talking to you!"

Stopping to look him in the eye, I reply, "Well, *Sir,* perhaps respect could also include the courtesy of not coming to my home unannounced, making demands you have no right to, and disquieting the neighborhood. Frankly, I am a busy woman and I have commitments that I must meet. This mess, as you call it, is promised to a young homeless person as a padding for her to sleep on, as she has no actual bed. I gave my word that it would be done by today, and if I am to keep my word, a currency I have worked hard to earn, I need to finish it. Is that ok with you?"

Taken aback by the stern tone of my response, he appears to back down a notch. "My apologies, ma'am, I suppose my desire to make progress on this mission has left my manners a bit short. I do still believe that this uniform stands for something, and the pride I hold in wearing it does not tend to accept anything less than the utmost respect."

I find people who demand respect are often not worthy of it. Looking up at the man who claims to be so proud of his uniform, I notice a couple of things that are why I don't quite believe him. Any soldier will remove their cover as soon as they enter a building, yet his soft cap is still in place over his

shaggy hair and several days' worth of beard. The full color flag, intended t
be on the right shoulder, is on the left, and would more likely be the gre
and black version used in field or combat situations. His uniform is sportin
a Chaplain's insignia, yet he carries a weapon, which is against militar
regulations as Chaplains are considered non-combatants. It would be unwis
to let on that I know he is a total fraud until the situation can be bette
evaluated.

"I agree that a soldier in uniform deserves great respect, and I apologiz
if you feel that I have not given it. Perhaps I can come outside with you an
meet your men."

"Sure, the sooner we can form an alliance, the sooner we can mov
forward and make a difference." The Captain moves to hold open the doo
for me to pass.

It's been a while since I've seen some of these vehicles. I used to tak
Matthew down to post to visit Cameron every so often. He was a Range
and went out to the field frequently. He taught me quite a bit abou
different aspects of the Army and even took us to visit a motor pool once t
see some of the heavy equipment, like the Stryker, that was almost in m
front yard. Beyond that, I see a couple of large trucks and a
honest-to-goodness tank.

"These vehicles are impressive! I'm surprised they are still around. W
were sure the base would have been destroyed in The Coming."

"A lot of it was, but a few buildings and vehicles were left intact." Th
Captain proudly replies.

"Well, I am impressed. I'd love to meet your men if you don't mind."

The Captain makes a cutting motion across his throat. "Shut 'em dow
and step on out, boys!"

Thankfully, the terrible racket filling the air disappeared as each of th
engines were shut off. Surprisingly, only one or two men came from each o
the quiet vehicles.

"Have you not been able to stop off anywhere else for recruits yet?"

"No ma'am, we hit the ground and came straight here."

"I see. Tell me about yourself, Soldier." Looking at what is supposed to be a specialist, who appears to be maybe eighteen or nineteen years old.

"Yes, ma'am. I am Specialist Joe Marks, Apache pilot taken to ground, now I drive this thing in an effort to help rebuild this crazy world."

"Very nice to meet you, Specialist Marks. I am sorry to hear that you are unable to fly, but I suppose the fuel would be hard to come by."

Wrong rank for a pilot and too young to be a Specialist anyway, another fake.

"And how about you?" Nodding to another very young man who had come down out of the Stryker.

"I am Private Jesse Ruiz, ma'am. I was stationed with an infantry division out of another post, but I was over this way for training when everything went down, so now I'm a part of this group instead."

"It is very nice to meet you, Private."

There is no need to see more. If there is a true soldier amongst this group, he is doing a terrible job of keeping this charade in line.

"Can I speak with you, Captain?" I say as I walk away from the vehicles enough to afford our conversation a bit of privacy.

He follows me about 10 feet from the first vehicle.

"So, I didn't want to call you guys out publicly if I can avoid it and I'm not sure if this is all just an elaborate ploy to get people to give you supplies, or what your game is, but unless you can tell me the truth, I'm going to have to ask you to move on."

"*Excuse* me! Are you questioning our honor?" The Captain's countenance has shifted from irritated to completely enraged.

"You can take it however you like, but the truth of the matter is that your stories are inaccurate, and I am unable to believe them. My brother was a soldier among the disappeared at the post I'm guessing you robbed before coming here. I don't think there is a true soldier among you, or he would not let such blatantly obvious errors stand."

"You think you're so smart, don't you? How smart are you now?"

As somewhat expected, he has pulled a pistol, and I am now looking down the barrel at the smug face of the lying man behind it. How I wish people would change... that honor and integrity would have a more common place in the world.

"BRUTE!"

"What's that supposed to me--?"

"Uhhh, Sir?"

Before the so-called Captain could finish his sentence, one or more people stepped out of every house on the street, even the houses up the steep hill directly behind my house. Each one is holding a rifle or pistol of some kind, all of them aimed at the band of men on the street.

"Please lower your gun so we can return to being civilized. You see, I may not be formally in charge, but I am responsible for each of these families and their ability to live in relative safety, and have food to eat. I am also the main healer. They do come to me with problems because I am fair and just when needed. If they do something wrong, they answer for it. If they need justice, I help them find it. I garden and teach others to as well. I broker deals with those who have what we do not. They will protect this house and each other fiercely, because we are a community here. We all look out for and rely on each other, and will each die to protect the rest if necessary. Can you say the same of your band of men? Do you want to die today? I don't, if it can be avoided. So you have a choice: surrender your weapons, and we will talk, or don't."

You would think this would be a simple decision to make; in fact, each of his men had already tossed down their weapons and had their hands above their heads without instruction. The look on the Captain's face reflected more of panic and anger as he started thinking hard, trying to find a way out of the mess he was now in. Slowly, he lowers his weapon.

"Yes, let's talk. May we go inside again? The street makes me a bit nervous now."

"Darryl, please collect the weapons while we get this all sorted out. I think everyone will feel a lot better knowing we aren't about to have an open battle in our front yard.

Captain, we can definitely go inside, but I will need you to leave your weapons outside with my neighbor. My living room is not quite big enough for everyone, but you can bring one or two in with you if you need to. I believe your men could also benefit from some water. I'll see if a neighbor can bring that to them as well."

Speaking a bit louder, "Can someone please bring some water out to these men? No reason we can't be hospitable."

Stepping inside, I motion to the loveseat and second chair in the living room as options for the outed Captain and what looks like a Sergeant Reyes before sitting back in the chair with my crochet mat project. I'm sure it will annoy this man again, but those kids could be here any minute.

"Please, have a seat. I truly hope that we can move past all of this, but it will require complete honesty. I need to know who you really are and what your true purpose is."

"You were right that we aren't actually soldiers. There was a man named Jerry I met a few weeks ago, who was in the reserves about ten years ago and was an Oathkeeper during that time. He isn't the most reliable person, which is why he isn't with us. I was able to get him to tell me some things, but obviously not enough to fool anyone but a complete civilian."

"I see, and what was the plan in coming here?"

"Look, you caught us. We aren't who we said we are, but it's not like we hurt anyone. I don't feel much like being interrogated by some woman." The Captain's arms are crossed, and he has leaned back into the chair, behaving much like you would expect of a student sent to the principal's office.

"Fair enough. One more question, then. What results are you hoping to have come from this conversation?"

"I already told you, we need recruits and supplies so we can go to the outlands and give these monsters a little hell. Give them to us, and everything will be just peachy."

I sigh, resigned to the fact that this part of the conversation isn't going to go any better than the first. "Well, I promised no more questions. There is a truck stop with a small hotel out on Route 80, as you head along the main road you turned off of to come in here. You can take your men there to wait until a decision can be made. Someone will come to you once that is done. I would ask that you respect our space and remain there peacefully, or move on should you decide not to wait. There is no reason for this to be any uglier than it already has been."

The Captain's snarky tone continues. "You don't give us orders, we are free to choose what we do, or do not do."

"You are correct, every person has free will. However, not every person has a weapon, and as you may recall, your men have been disarmed. If staying in a relatively decent hotel doesn't work for you, you are welcome to stay in our local jail while you wait instead. That is definitely a choice you can make. Threatening us, or otherwise proving to act outside of the common laws that have been adopted here, may serve to remove that decision from you."

Standing quickly, the men start towards the door, but not before the Captain raises a finger towards me, obviously angered by his loss of power.

"I see this conversation isn't going anywhere, so we'll go to your hick hotel, but I'm not going to sit around and wait very long. You better not try to keep me waiting either if you know what's good for you."

The men walk outside, slamming the door. It is only a moment before the sound of diesels has faded and the neighborhood is quiet once more. If only my thoughts were as well.

After The Coming

Chapter Six

Decisions, Decisions

With the soldiers gone, several neighbors come over and gather in a small circle in my front yard to find out what was going on. Mama Lou from a couple of doors down, Jed and his son Brandon from across the street, Marsha from next door to Jed, Tom and Brian, my neighbors on either side, then Joshua, strangely, appeared as well. *How long has he been back in town?*

Tom is the first to speak. "So what do those men want from us?"

Marsha says in a worried tone. "I didn't like the looks of them one bit!"

"Maybe we oughta jus' go shoot 'em and be done with it!" Brandon is 17, and his voice is full of typical teenage invincibility.

"Ok, ok, let's just settle down for a minute before a noose and pitchforks come out! I've learned quite a bit about them so far, and I honestly don't like what I have seen. The men are not soldiers, they are a group that has formed with the idea of stopping at a few towns, collecting supplies and recruits to go fight in the outlands. It is frankly suicide, and I have no intention of recommending any of our people go with them.

The leader does not seem to be the most stable, though, so this needs to be handled carefully. I know we took the guns that were obvious, but I don't know if they carry shells for the big guns, or if the presence of their vehicles is supposed to bluff them through. Either way, I think they are dangerous. I've asked them to wait out at the old hotel on 80 for us to discuss this and make a decision."

The neighbors who gathered aren't a formal council, but not much gets done on the hillside without at least one of us knowing about it.

"So like I said, let's sneak over there and shoot 'em all while they sleep then." Brandon's puffed-up chest and hands perched on his hips increase his size, but not his wisdom.

My arms cross in front of me as if to block the thought being shared.

"Brandon, killing people for what they *might* do is murder and is completely out of the question." I shake my head in frustration. *I hope he starts to pick up some sense coming into these meetings.*

Tom looks around the group with a raised brow and crossed arms of his own. "I agree that they don't sound like anything good, and I'm definitely not keen on just handing them things. People like that don't tend to be satisfied with a little if they think they can, or should have a lot."

"Excellent point, Tom. Do you have any suggestions as to a safe way to send them along peacefully without giving in to their demands in a way that might bring them back?" I ask.

The beauty of a group is that sometimes it doesn't all have to rest on me to solve every problem myself.

"Sadly, no, this is definitely a pickle!" Tom shakes his head, looking down as he kicks a small bunch of grass.

"What if we tell the Sheriff and let him deal with it. Maybe if we're lucky, they'll take each other out and make everyone safer all around." Poor

Marsha asks, still so afraid of everything. It's little wonder her hair is mostly grey, even though she is barely into her 40s.

"While I do agree that the Sheriff isn't the safest person either, and will likely require some sort of intervention if things continue the way they are, I fear he would just be kerosene to this fire."

After a thoughtful pause, Jed speaks up. "What if we give them some rations and their weapons back, with the understanding that they are not welcome to return, and should they return, they will be met with force?"

"I can see your point, Jed, but I can't help but be concerned about those still living isolated out on the farms. Here we can protect each other, but it would not be hard for this group to overrun one or more of the farmhouses out there. We depend on them for a lot of the provisions that come into town. I suppose I am just afraid that any further issues with them will come back at us violently. Like I said, the Captain does not appear to be very stable or logical in his actions."

"Well then, Miss Ray, whatcha want us to do 'bout it then?" As much as I love Mama Lou, it never ceases to amaze me how young she can make me feel.

"I wish I had a magic answer. To be sure, this feels like an impossible situation. Perhaps we should take a bit to think about it, and then come back together this evening."

"I suppose, but those men best stay out of town. I get the feelin' they's up to no good regardless."

"Sadly, I agree, Mama Lou. We'll be back maybe an hour before sundown." Jed and Brandon pick up the weapons they had collected from the men and turn back toward their house.

"Thanks, everyone."

As the neighbors leave, I remember Joshua is there. He's been silent this whole time, and I find myself hoping he might have an idea.

"I didn't expect to see you again so soon. Have you been in town this whole time?"

"Yes, I was finishing up a couple of things I needed to do down here when I saw the trucks rolling through. When I saw them heading this way, I followed them here, but figured I should wait and see what happened. You handled it all quite admirably, considering what you were facing. I think you are right about those men being bad news."

"The whole thing is such a mess. I truly wish they had just never come to town, but that isn't helpful. Do you have any thoughts on a peaceful way to send them along?"

"Possibly, but in reality, does it do anyone any good to pass them on to the next town? I mean, not everyone is going to see them for what they are. What happens when they bully someone into arming them further, and making them stronger? There is no guarantee that they will abide by an agreement and not come back with more men and firepower later."

"I wish you didn't make so much sense right now. If I'm being honest, the only way to ensure anything is to disarm them completely and either put them to work in the community or jail them, but that doesn't really help anything. They have not yet done anything wrong, and it is not our place to be judge and jury over someone just because they make us uncomfortable.

On the other hand, can we afford to wait until they do something malicious before allowing a reaction where people may honestly be hurt or killed? This whole thing is just a disaster waiting to happen, and I feel like nothing I do is going to be right!"

Walking back into the house, I drop myself into my favorite chair with a thud and hide my face in my hands, hoping that by rubbing my eyes I just might see things more clearly.

"That's a lot of pressure for one person to try to handle. I agree that the situation is complicated, but I also think that it isn't just on you to make any huge decisions here." Joshua's thoughtful concern is etched across his brow as he mirrors my position from the loveseat across the tiny living room.

"Ok, that may be true," I respond, looking up at Joshua, still leaning forward with my arms on my knees.

"It's also true that I currently speak for at least this part of town in this matter, and these people are expecting me to come up with a solution. Meanwhile, there is a group of potentially very dangerous people barely outside of town waiting for an answer that I don't have!"

"Ray, I understand that you feel responsible here, and I have great respect for that. I also think that you need to relax a bit so that you can stop and see the situation from the outside. If this were a problem on a board and none of the people had faces, what would your instinct tell you to do?" Joshua's soothing tone and quiet demeanor are exactly what I need to try to figure this out.

"I don't know... Maybe speak to all of the men and offer them a place here in the town to stay with us, then find them work, maybe helping in the jail or wherever their talents may lie, and then keep the equipment here as part of the town's defense against others like them. That leaves the problem of the possibility that they may try to earn our trust and then hurt us later, though. Ugh! Why do things have to be so hard?"

I didn't realize I was up and pacing again until Joshua came up and set his hands on my shoulders to stop me from moving.

"It's going to be ok. We'll figure this out. Let's make some tea and talk about something else for a bit."

I sigh, resigned to his wisdom. "Ok, but just for a few minutes. This has to be a priority."

"It is a priority, just trust me, ok?" His earnest face and kind eyes sit perfectly over the start of a smile tugging one corner of his mouth upward.

"Yeah, ok. What would you like in your tea?"

"Don't worry about it, I'll fix some for both of us." He says as he starts walking into the kitchen. "I want you to sit in this chair and finish your mat. Those kids will be here any time, won't they?"

"Ugh, you're right! Shoot!" I smack my forehead with the heel of my palm, once again reminded that my task is waiting.

Thankfully, I only have a few more rows, so I can finish this pretty quickly. I glance over my shoulder to see Joshua making himself right at home in the kitchen. Looking at the counter, I can see chamomile flowers going into one cup and peppermint leaves in the other. It's nice to see him so comfortable with herbs. *I wonder where he learned that.*

Quietly coming up behind me, Joshua slips the cup onto the little side table beside my chair.

"Here is a nice cup of chamomile tea. Now, why don't you tell me a bit about the ideas you mentioned for those boneheads up on the mountain?"

"You do know that *you* live up there, too, right?" I can't help but chuckle as Joshua retakes his spot on the loveseat across from me.

Joshua laughs as well. "Of course I do, but I am obviously not a bonehead, except when it comes to trying to talk to those old fools and make any sort of difference." His light mood takes on a hint of sadness.

I look Joshua in the eyes, hoping to convey my sincerity. "I'm sorry, I'm sure that must be very frustrating. I didn't mean to make light of it."

Joshua shakes his head briefly. "You're fine, I suppose I am a touch testy about the subject. I've been trying for years to make improvements and suggest changes, but I am consistently met with odd looks, excuses, and ridicule. You didn't offend me at all; I can see the humor in it." His statement was accentuated with a little smile.

"I still apologize, and I would love to discuss a few ideas with you. I had a decent look at the soil up there, and I think there is real potential for both crops and livestock if it is managed well. Growing either or both of those kinds of food would not only affect the food shortage, but also provide your people with bartering power, which could serve to help add some modernization to the area." I look back down at my work as I continue.

"Part of the reason this house stays fed is that I have provided many people with seeds and food from my garden, but I also teach people how to dig wells, and my family's store had the hand pumps for the wells that have gone in, among other skills and trades.

I brokered a deal with a few farms that border my family's farm that have been selling us things we can't grow well in town, but it is limited and after the initial offerings of seed and such from the store, there isn't a whole lot else we have to offer them that they need. Mostly, it has been labor trades where several of the younger people go to the farms and live there for periods to learn and work. In return, the farm sends back a predetermined amount to their community. People take turns, with the exception of a few who don't care to be in town and would work either way." I glance up at Joshua to see that he seems thoughtful and interested in what I am sharing, so I continue.

"It's possible that we can find a trade that would prove helpful to both of our communities. I could talk to some of those who have experience with what I am talking about and maybe send up a few people to help get it started as an initial step in an agreement.

The best part about you all having more food is the end to that insane numbers lottery! My heart hurts for those who have experienced walking into that barn and been killed, for those who have lived and wondered why, and for the families burying their loved ones. The constant heartache of the people involved at any level must be crushing, even above the lack of resources leading to such a drastic measure." My face is lowered both from sadness and to try to finish the task at hand.

"It is horrendous. I think it is part of why things stay so backward. It's like this huge shadow has crossed over, and no one can see that there is sunlight if they would just move over a bit." Joshua shakes his head, obviously bothered by the reality of it all.

"I can't imagine what it must be like to live with that." I look back up at him with sincerity and empathy, knowing what a toll this must take on him.

"It's depressing and frustrating. I like the idea of it being over, though. What other thoughts have you had?" Joshua is leaning comfortably back in his seat, still sipping his peppermint tea, and obviously engaged in thought.

Continuing my work, I look back down at my hands, pushing hard to crochet quickly while still picturing what I saw and what it could look like.

"I think the soil is actually pretty decent, maybe a little rocky, but not too bad otherwise. With some hard work, I think a few areas could be cleared and amended for crops. Any wood that is cut down can be used for fences for the livestock, or buildings, the same with the larger rocks.

If the grasses were to be used to pasture some animals, starting with goats or sheep, then maybe chickens, they would do a lot of the prep work for you. Once they've moved through to other pastures, you could put some additional compost down from all the small tree waste, leaves, and other things left from the clearing to mulch and finish breaking down in place. Any ash left from burning can also be spread lightly, which would help clean up any wood-burning areas or stoves as well. With all of those amendments, that land would be perfect to start some winter crops for sure, but more likely some spring crops next year. I wish there was more that could be done immediately, but it is getting really late in the growing season to get much out of a summer crop harvest. It may be possible to build a greenhouse, though. I've been working on one here, actually. I want to try it out this year, and if it works the way I hope, we will ideally build more next spring as well."

"What are you building them out of?" Joshua's curiosity piqued.

"We have been collecting large glass inserts from screen doors and sliding doors first, and windows from buildings that are unlivable but still have intact glass here or there. A few windows are redirected to houses that need little to be whole again to help with the housing needs, but the rest all go to the greenhouse projects. Eventually, I want to see one on every other street at a minimum, but that's a lot of glass. We will probably end up having to make a few with rolled plastic, but I want to try to use glass as much as we can. So far, we have one greenhouse that is about 20 feet by 30 feet. It won't be enough to make everyone fat and happy, but I think we can keep people from starving."

Joshua nods, "That definitely would take a lot, but you could use wood and siding for the bottom few feet to help stretch the glass."

"Oh, for sure. The trick is harvesting large enough pieces that are in good shape without too many holes from previous use. I don't want to take away fragments from any good structures, and the ones that burned don't have a whole lot of decent material left.

I also have one farm in particular that has put up an amazing field full of winter wheat, one of barley, and another of oats. We're going to reserve enough grain to replant twice as much next year, but it is a lot of very hard work, and doing it practically by hand takes a lot of people.

From what I can see, you guys have a lot of hands up there. I really think that with just a little bit of guidance, and someone like you who has a higher ability for applying logic, for one thing, could really turn around." I smile and glance up to see if he has caught my intended meaning.

"Well, I appreciate the compliment, but I'm not sure they will. I've tried to bring up a lot of the things you have said here, and it just doesn't go well. They think that I am strange because I choose to read and use complete sentences. I'm not saying that I am unwilling to try, just that I wouldn't get my hopes up too far just yet. Although, to be fair, what you have accomplished here is truly amazing!" Joshua leans forward to lean his elbows onto his knees, hands clasped straight in front of him, and a look of sincere admiration on his face.

"I'm sorry that they haven't been very receptive, and I also thank you for the compliment. I just want to see people doing well, things being fixed, and life finding a reasonable normal. There is so much that is broken, and I just want to fix it." My tone is somber despite the compliment. This is such a heavy thought.

"That is very admirable. I would really like to help however I can."

"I'll hold you to that, you know?" Joshua's heartfelt support is encouraging and leaves me feeling just a bit playful.

A big grin takes over Joshua's face, "I'm counting on it!"

Chapter Seven

The Homeless Come Home

ap tap tap. The gentlest knock came at the door. I almost couldn't hear it over our conversation. Joshua turns to look out the window. "It's a couple of children, a boy and a girl, I'm guessing they're your homeless kids, do you want me to let them in?"

"Yes, please, I have just a tiny bit left."

He stands and turns before opening the door. "What are their names?"

"Isabelle and Franklin."

Opening the door, Joshua smiles and addresses the kids, "Hi, you must be Isabelle and Franklin. My name is Joshua. Miss Ray is inside. Would you like to come in?"

Franklin instinctively stepped between Joshua and Isabelle when the door opened with his chest puffed up as much as possible, even though he is younger and much shorter than she is. He takes a moment and skeptically looks Joshua up and down before answering, "Yeah, ok."

I call out from my seat, "Hey guys, I'm almost done with the second one. I'm so sorry to keep you waiting. Things around here have been a bit hectic the last couple of days. Are you hungry or thirsty at all? I have plenty of water, and some fresh tomatoes if you'd like to go out back and pick a few."

"Oh, could we?" Franklin's tough guy act melts completely at the promise of fresh food, and Isabelle is almost out the back door before I can answer. My heart hurts so much for what these children are going through. It would be a lot for an adult, but I've seen some as young as four out on the streets. They seem to find older children to help them, but it must still be so hard.

Looking at Joshua, who has just closed the front door, I ask, "Do you mind giving them a hand? I'm not sure how much they know about plants."

Joshua chuckles. "Sure, how many do you want them to take?"

"Oh, have them each eat a big one and take a few with them. There are plenty of green ones on to replace any they take."

This should keep them busy for the few more minutes I need to finish the second mat.

Joshua follows the children out the back door as I finish the last half row of the mat. It takes only a few minutes before the back door opens and the children run in excitedly. "Miss Ray, these are the best tomatoes I ever ate!"

"I'm glad you like them, Franklin. I like them too. Did you guys pack a few for later?"

"Yes, ma'am, Mr. Joshua helped us pick some good ones!" Franklin excitedly replies.

"That makes me happy, then. Why don't you two come over here and tell me a bit about how you are and where you've been staying?" I've just rolled up the finished mat and tied it closed with a strip of crocheted plarn that also serves as a shoulder carry strap, and set it with the first on the floor next to my chair.

"The other kids won't like it if we tell Miss Ray, that's one of the rules." Isabelle's light mood shifted so quickly that I almost regret starting this conversation, but it needs to be had.

"Oh? Are they afraid someone will tell you that you can't be there anymore?" I ask, thoughtfulness etching my brow.

"Yeah, I don't think we are supposed to be where we are, but so far, there hasn't been anyone to tell us we can't be there, and it is a nice enough place."

"Do you feel safe there?" My concern is apparent and seems to be received well.

"Most of the time. A couple of the older kids run things and can get pretty mean sometimes." Isabelle looks down at the floor as she speaks, not used to being so open.

"I don't like the way they look at Isabelle. I tell them I'm gonna fight them if they try to touch her." The young boy pounds his fist into his other hand in a moment of bravado.

Embarrassed, Isabelle yells at him, "Shut up, Franklin!"

"Why? It's not like she's gonna tell anyone." Yelling back, Franklin gestures towards me with an open hand.

"Thank you for the tomatoes and mats, Miss Ray, but we really need to go." Isabelle is already standing and trying to pull Franklin along with her.

Looking at Joshua, I scramble for a way to keep the children just a few more minutes. "Joshua, would you be so kind as to take Franklin out back again? I think there may be some carrots about ready to pick and maybe even an early melon."

"Sure, I can do that." He stands and starts to walk towards the back door. "Would you like to come with me, Franklin?"

Waiting for the guys to close the back door, I try again.

"Isabelle, I'm sorry, I didn't mean to upset you. I was only asking these things because I worry about all of you, and I want to do what I can to help.

I've had a few ideas, and I was hoping maybe you could help me with them. Would you be willing to listen to them and let me know what you think?"

Isabelle sighs and sits back down. "I guess, but no more questions, ok?"

"I will try to limit them to exactly what I would need to know for the ideas, and you can refuse to answer if it is too uncomfortable. Fair enough?"

She shrugs, "Yeah, alright."

"Thank you, I really appreciate it. I have been trying to figure out a way to maybe open the high school back up with a new purpose. Instead of focusing solely on classwork and books like it did before, I'd like to try to convert some of the rooms into dorm rooms with beds and everything for children whose parents haven't been found. Siblings would have the option to stay together. Otherwise, it would be girls in an area with other girls, and boys with other boys in separate hallways.

I'm thinking that if we can get a bunch of older kids together, we can look at collecting bunk beds and other beds from houses that are abandoned, starting with the ones that may not be livable anymore anyway, and transport them. If we use three of the halls as the dorms, and the rest for the classes, then everyone would still be able to be together. What do you think so far?"

Isabelle pauses before responding, brow furrowed in contemplation. "There's a couple of older kids that Franklin mentioned that would be the big ones to convince. They pretty much run things, and they scare the other kids, so no one is going to want to do anything they say no to."

"Ok, that's helpful. Do you think there is a way I can meet with these older kids, somewhere neutral, maybe so it doesn't give away where you are staying?"

"Maybe, they don't really listen to us, so I'm not sure I can get them to do anything." Isabelle's arms cross, irritated at the lack of control she has.

"I understand, we can work out a plan for that in a bit. Another part of the idea would be to bring in some adults from the community with different useful skills to teach classes, so that, especially the older kids, can learn things that would give them the chance to have a job later. Things like construction, farming, engineering, cooking, understanding of electricity, which I hope to be able to bring back eventually, how to raise animals, and such.

Some children may even be given a rotation out to a couple of farms to learn these things, which would, in turn, help to supply food to the group as payment for their help. There may be more than this depending on the skills of any adults I find who are willing to help." I watch Isabelle carefully to see if she will show any tells as to what she thinks of each of these ideas.

Isabelle shrugs, pushing her hands under her thighs on the couch. "Some of that could be good if you can get the kids to do it. A lot of kids are really happy that there isn't school anymore. Some of them even talk about burning it down."

My brow furrows in concern, "Well, that isn't going to help. Does it sound like any of them have any real plans to do that?"

Isabelle shrugs again and looks down and away from my gaze. "I don't think so, but you never know. They do some pretty stupid things sometimes."

"Hmm, ok. It sounds like maybe I need to try to make this a bigger priority. Would you be willing to find out a couple of things for me?"

"I don't know, I don't think they'll listen to me." Isabelle wraps her arms around herself and looks away.

"I have an idea. Maybe don't keep all of the food I'm sending with you a secret. Let them find out you have it, and when they ask you where you got it, you can tell them you have a friend who gave it to you. Tell them that I would be willing to give them a bit for themselves if they will meet me in two days, around lunchtime, out front of the high school."

She looks back at me with wide eyes. "That breaks another rule. I have to bring it straight to them anyway. The older kids choose who eats what."

Frustration crosses my features. "That's not very nice. Please come by anytime if you need something to eat. I don't have a lot, but I'll see that you get something.

As far as the rules, don't fight them. If they want to take all of what you bring back, let them. I don't want either of you to get hurt. One of the most important parts of this is that I need you to tell them that you don't know where the food comes from because you usually meet me in the alley near The Restaurant. They may be young, but I doubt that they would be foolish enough to try anything at Lalonda's place. Do you think you would be able to do that for me?"

"I think so. What if they try to hurt me, or Franklin, though? I have to protect him." Isabelle is obviously scared of these older boys, as made apparent by the wide-eyed look growing as she considers her options.

"That's why I don't want you to fight. If they press, just stick to the story that you don't know where I live. From here on, if you do need to come by, maybe come in the back gate, it's fairly well hidden and would not be as obvious."

Isabelle is still afraid, understandably so. "I'm not sure I want to do this."

"It's a lot to ask, I know, and I wouldn't if I saw a better option. I think you are right that I need to get them on board before anything big can be done to help, and it'll be getting cold again in just a few months. You guys need beds, warm clothes, and food if you are going to make it ok. I just want to help any way that I can."

Isabella takes a thoughtful moment before nodding. "Thank you, Miss Ray. I'll see what I can do. We need to go now, though."

"Thank you, Isabelle. You are such a strong young lady. I am so proud of how you take care of Franklin. Be safe on your way back."

"We will."

I follow Isabelle to the back door as she grabs the mats and steps outside to collect Franklin, as well as a few more veggies. They are out the back gate quickly, and Joshua comes to join me at the back door.

"That boy can chat up a storm!" Joshua's lighthearted comment comes with a sweet smile.

"Joshua, do you think you could do me a favor?" I ask, thoughtfully considering my conversation with Isabelle.

"Sure, anything." Joshua, still in a light mood, is openly receptive to my request.

"Can you see if you can follow them without them knowing and figure out where they're going?"

"Will do, I'll be back as soon as I can." Joshua winks as he turns and jogs for the gate.

"Thank you!" I call after him.

Just like that, he was out the back, right behind them. *I hope he can follow them without being discovered. I worry about those two. I worry about all of them.*

Chapter Eight

Off To Work

BRRRIIIINNNNGGGG! Who knew an alarm clock could be a welcome sound? Most mornings of late, I've been woken up before the silly thing had a chance to do its job. Hearing it now means I actually slept until 6 AM for once.

Growing up on the farm, Daddy was usually my alarm clock. He would wake me up with some random little poem, then whistle off to do a couple of chores while Mama made breakfast. Cameron was terrible about getting out of bed, and Daddy wasn't always so kind about getting him up after asking for the third or fourth time. I wasn't the greatest fan of the hour either, but I loved being out with him, smelling the crisp morning air, saying good morning to all of the barn animals, just getting up themselves, and also hungry for breakfast.

Farm life definitely wasn't glamorous, but there was something special about those early mornings, the way the sun broke over the fields, the fresh dew on the grass, the way that one silly rooster crowed funny after his run-in with the mean old barn cat. Everyone had a purpose and a place, a design for their lives, and a common Creator who saw it all. It may take hard work, but it's happy work if you let it be.

Some days, I wish I were back there, waking up to the sweet smells of coffee, turkey bacon, and fresh hay each day. Today is not that day, though. Today, Jamal and I have to get to work on the library at The Restaurant and face the not-so-sweet reality of Lalonda.

Since I have some time before we have to be there, I decide to take the chance to put in a little work in the garden. It's needed a good weeding and some real watering for a while now. Thankfully, God has been raining on it for me a lot lately, so the plants are all in good shape. While I'm outside, I hear the door open, and see Matthew.

"Hey, Auntie, can I help?"

"Of course, Bud, come over and I'll show you which plants we want to take out."

"Ok!" Matthew runs over to where I am kneeling in the grass.

This sweet boy has no idea just how much he looks like his father did at this age.

"Ok, so you see these ones that are long, thin, and smooth?" I ask, pointing to a clump of grass.

"Yeah."

"These are a type of grass and will try to take over if we let it, so you want to carefully grab the whole bunch right down at the bottom making sure you don't get the feathery carrot top right next to it at the same time then pull straight up, like this." I easily pull out a decent bunch from the moist soil. "Then, you gently shake it off and put as much of the soil back down as you can. It's full of everything we need to grow our veggies, so we want to keep every bit we can, ok?"

Matthew grabs a big bunch and, surprisingly, after much straining, pulls it out, dropping himself back on his backside from the effort.

A full belly laugh escapes, and I ask, "Are you ok?"

"I'm ok, did you see that? I knew I could do it!" Matthew's innocent excitement is almost palpable as he bears a huge smile and shows off his dirty prize.

"And you did! I'm very proud of you!" Offering a hand, I help him stand up and give him a quick side hug.

"Thanks, Auntie! Can we go see Mama Lou now? Kevin is supposed to be coming again today, and I told him I would bring him a surprise."

"Oh? And what did you have in mind?"

Matthew grins. "I want to bring him a strawberry if you say it's alright."

"Of course it is, how about that one right there?" Pointing at a lovely, large, red berry hiding under several leaves.

"That one looks good! I bet he'll smile when he sees that!" The joy on his face is infectious, and a lovely boost to start out what promises to be a difficult day.

I playfully tousle Matthew's hair. "You're such a sweet boy, Matthew. Let's grab your berry and head over to Mama Lou's."

"Ok!"

*****

It only takes a couple of minutes to walk up the street to Mama Lou's, but before we even get close, it is apparent that something is amiss.

"Matthew, stay behind me, ok?"

"Yes, ma'am." Matthew quickly steps behind me, still following closely.

"I said, where is the boy?"

Seeing Lalonda's pink Cadillac on the curb, that shouting is no doubt coming from one of her men.

"An' I told *you*, he ain't here, now get yo'self back up off ma porch." Mama Lou's hands are on her hips, and she is leaning slightly forward in a defensive posture that I wouldn't want to mess with. These men aren't known to be all that smart, though.

"Maybe we will just come on in and have a look for ourselves." The larger man of the two takes a couple more steps up onto the porch as if to enter the home.

"No, you ain't doin' that!"

I could tell Mama Lou was scared, but I'm not sure who was more afraid at that moment, her, or the men she was shoving off the porch with the broom she just grabbed from its resting place by the door. The woman was not one to be messed with, especially when it comes to someone she cares about.

I turn and quietly issue an order, "Matthew, run up beside the house and in the back door quickly. Go inside and find Miss Lola, and I'll see you later tonight, ok?"

"Ok." He runs off and is out of sight before I can make it the last 40 feet to the front of Mama Lou's house.

"What exactly is going on here?" I ask with all the authority I can muster.

"This crazy old lady is assaulting us!" The smaller of the men shouts out from behind his partner.

"I ain't done no such thing... yet! You was trespassin', and threatenin' and I am jus' defendin' mine."

The larger man adds, "We just came to pick up the boy for work is all and she started hollering and beating us!"

Putting my hands up in front of me to try to pause the situation, I sternly counter, "Ok, ok! For one, Mama Lou told you the truth, Jamal isn't here, and you have no right to insinuate that she was lying or attempting to force your way into her home. Secondly, who do you think you are to be allowed to present yourselves this way? You hold no special power or rights up here, and you will behave respectfully towards anyone you encounter from here on out, is that understood?"

"Yeah."

"Ok." Each of the men responds, dejected after their scolding.

"Close enough. If you really do intend to provide a ride for Jamal, he is at my house, and I will be coming with him. If you pull your car around, I will go inside and get him ready. We are still over an hour from when we are due to start working, so you will need to wait for a bit. Fair enough?" My hands on my hips further serve to accentuate the tone I'm using.

"Yeah, alright." The smaller man replies sullenly.

"Before you leave, I suggest you sincerely apologize to Mama Lou for your vulgar and abhorrent actions."

Both heads hanging, the larger one speaks up, "Sorry, ma'am, we shouldn't have acted like that."

"Thank ya' for the sorry, now git on outta 'ere and don' y'all come back." Mama Lou, still brandishing her broom, pops it out away from her, just to be sure they got the point.

"Yes, ma'am." A chorus of murmured replies comes together as the men hang their heads in obvious shame from the scolding they just received. If I didn't know better, I'd think I was dealing with a couple of school boys instead of life-hardened, grown men.

"Good, we will be out shortly," I say as I walk past the men toward the porch.

The men silently trudge to the car, start it, and head up the street to turn around before parking in front of my house.

Heading up to Mama Lou, she is visibly relaxing. I place a hand on her shoulder, concern filling my face after seeing her so upset.

"Mama, are you ok?"

"Yeah, jus' flustered is all. Who do they think they is comin' 'roun' here like they own me, or my Jamal?" Mama Lou moves away and sets the broom back down by the door.

"I agree, and I think you handled yourself well. I hope they will realize their place, but just in case, pass the word to keep an eye out for any trouble. I sent Matty around the house and told him to go in your back door. I hope that's ok. I wasn't sure how this was going to play out."

Mama Lou nods, "Tha's fine, I wasn't too sure myself." A relieved smile begins to cross her face.

"Oh! Matty brought a strawberry for Kevin. I think it really bothers him that he can't get the boy to smile."

"Yeah, I been workin' on 'im, but he is jus' a crabby one. Not sure berry is gonna change that any." Mama's arms cross, thinking about Kevin.

"Well, I wanted to let him try his idea anyway. Not enough sweet souls around anymore, I'd like to try to help him keep his as long as possible."

"True 'nough."

Arriving back at the house, the two men are sitting quietly in the Cadillac. Hopefully, this sort of calm continues, as I still don't know which men beat Jamal so terribly the other night. I hope he doesn't remember either now that he will be there with them all day, every day. I haven't gotten him up yet, so I grab some tea I started for him earlier and pour it into thermos before I head back to the spare room. I knock softly before opening the door.

"Good morning, Jamal, how are you doing?"

Jamal opens his eyes slightly, wincing as he takes a deeper breath. "I'm hurtin', Miss Ray, hurtin' pretty bad."

"I expect that will be the case for a while, Jamal, and for that I'm sorry. The good news is we have a ride to take us to work today, so that will help. I have made you some healing tea to take with, it should take some of the edge off." I raise the thermos for Jamal to see.

"Thanks, Miss Ray."

"Now let's get to the Library and get the place spruced up!" I say with an enthusiasm made purely from will power.

Chapter Nine

New Beginnings

Pulling up to The Restaurant was thankfully uneventful. I helped Jamal inside and slowly lowered him into one of the overstuffed chairs that had been brought over with the shelves collected to make the library space. Lalonda's men had brought everything in yesterday from the back room of my family's store and really just put it down without any sort of order. I wish I had been here to direct them so things wouldn't all have to be moved again, but I can't be everywhere at once.

The tables and chairs in the front corner of the dining room have all been shifted over into the remaining space, or out of the room entirely, making an area large enough to fit the pile of empty bookshelves that have been dumped there. I quickly get to work rearranging shelves based on the space we have. The corner and one wall of this space do not have windows, so I move the taller shelves up against the wall on that side first. There are a few shorter shelves that I shift to create a half wall of sorts, closing off the space as its own area and making a lot more room to sort through and organize the books once Joshua can bring them back down. The taller shelves are a mixture of wood finishes, all gathered from empty houses around town. They are all about 6 feet tall, so it still seems purposeful.

The shorter shelves are all black and came from a daycare building that had experienced a fire during The Coming but were not damaged. They are all a little dirty and smell just a tiny bit like smoke, so I take some damp rags and begin to wipe away the dirt and dust. As they come clean, it is almost like I am taking them back through time, to a place before everything became so hard.

There are only two, royal blue, plush armchairs for now, so one will go in the corner facing out next to the big windows, and the other on the opposite side of a small mahogany side table. The chairs came from a realtor's office just up the street, as well as the side table. They are easily the nicest things in the space and really class it up a bit compared to the vinyl and veneered tables in the dining room area. Ideally, Jamal will sit here in one of the chairs during the day, and we can create a catalog to sit there as well. *I think there was a carpenter on the list of skilled people left in the community, maybe he can build us something for that.*

A sour voice cuts through my thoughts. "I thought your pet was supposed to be doing the work."

My eyes briefly close tightly shut at the sound of Lalonda's voice, thankfully coming from behind me, so she doesn't see my reaction to her presence. I figured she would come over eventually, but I was not looking forward to it.

I turn around to face her, trying hard to control my feelings, at least on the outside. "He would be had he not had a run-in with a few men who felt the need to beat him half to death a couple of nights ago. I am just making sure that things go smoothly here. After all, you did say I would be responsible for his debt if he wasn't able to pay it."

"It's no skin off my nose if you want to work for free, I'm not feeding both of you, though." Her pointed finger leaves no doubt about the truth in her words.

I fight to maintain a polite tone, despite my internal frustration. "I didn't expect you to. I'm about finished here until the books arrive anyway. I invited a couple of people from neighboring towns to come by today to discuss a business venture with you. I think you will be very pleased with the potential benefits of the conversation."

"Ex*cuse* me? You just spring this on me without any warning? Who do you think you are, inviting people to *my* place of business without permission?" Her entitled arms cross as she leans back to accentuate the vitriol in her voice.

I sigh in resignation. It is never an easy conversation here. "You're right, Lalonda, I should have mentioned it before. With all of the chaos lately, it slipped my mind. Would you like to discuss it for a bit before they arrive so you are more prepared for the meeting?"

"You *think*? How am I supposed to plan what I want from these people if I don't even know what I'm talking about?" The selfishness dripping from Lalonda's words and tone is so opposite from everything I stand for that it is difficult to want to continue. If she didn't have something we needed, I would never want to include her in such talks.

"Absolutely, would you like to talk in your booth?"

"Might as well." Lalonda gestures with sweeping arms towards her favorite seat.

Making our way to the old, red vinyl, round booth in the back corner of the main room would only take a moment and I find myself wishing it would take just a bit longer as I try to prepare an approach to this in a way that will make her think she is getting the best side of the deal, since that's the only chance we have at a successful meeting with her involved.

Sliding into the seat across from her, I begin, "I found some old maps recently that show our town and the surrounding area, including the towns on either side of us. Did you know that there is an old plane scrap yard in Harrison, to the west of us?"

"No, but what does it matter? Are you going to start building planes now?" *Does everything require sarcasm?*

"No-o-o, I have something else in mind. I also found that there is a manufacturing plant in Carlsburg to the east. I think if we can make a deal with both towns, we may be able to rig up some windmill electricity generators. The leaders we would need to deal with from those two towns are the ones I have invited here today." I clasp my hands together on top of the table, hoping to control them and my temper at the same time.

"My thought is that you have a few large trucks that still work, Harrison has the parts, and Carlsburg has the people with experience and the machinery to build a series of windmills to help us generate electricity for our towns. I can manage all of the deals to get the pieces in place, and then get the finished sets where they need to go, which is why we are all meeting today."

"Yes, I do have the trucks, so it sounds like none of this happens without me, so I want the windmill right here for my use, then." Lalonda leans back with her arm across the back of the booth seat. Her typical snarky tone is no surprise, nor is her desire to take every advantage possible.

"Really, none of this happens without everyone working together, but by doing so, we all benefit. If everything is split with a third of the items going to each town, then we each gain something for our towns that we could not manage by ourselves. This plan would work out a way to potentially have a whole field of them by the time we're done, if I can. From a logistical standpoint, it doesn't make sense to put them in random locations around town, but rather near the old power station so the electricity can be managed using the existing infrastructure."

Lalonda Interrupts, placing her hands on her chest. "So what I hear you saying is that I use my trucks, my gas, and then I have to share with everyone else?"

"To a degree, yes. The trucks are definitely yours. The gas would be used from the town reserves, so that would not cost you your rations, and yes, everyone would eventually benefit from the project. I have asked a couple of men who used to work for the electric company to go through town and disconnect the individual power lines to any homes that are too damaged to be livable, and they are also cutting them to any buildings that are currently abandoned. This will help keep the draw on the power that is generated down. From there, we will have to work out how to manage the power that is used so we don't have a bunch of people trying to turn on AC units and refrigerators, then crashing the grid.

In short, this doesn't work without you, and think of how well people will think of you for doing this. It would definitely be a great reflection on you as far as the areas of our community go, and after the whole mess with Jamal recently, a little goodwill could make a real difference." I hope playing to her ego will help convince her to cooperate. Trying to move the parts with smaller vehicles is a challenge I would rather avoid.

"I don't really care what people think of me, if they don't see by now that I am the boss around here, then they would be too stupid to know whether this helps them or not. Why should I share with people that dumb? No, if I do this, I want the power here first." Lalonda presses her pointed fingertip down onto the worn tabletop for emphasis.

I shift in my seat, trying to work out a way to help Lalonda see past her selfishness to understand the bigger picture. "The biggest problem with that is managing the power and making it usable. Wind energy is not a constant, so it needs to be managed with equipment capable of handling the fluctuation without burning out. Then it needs to go through a process to turn the energy into something that is usable with the systems that are already in place. Once that has happened, there has to be a system in place to store the energy that is not immediately being used for the time when the output is too low to meet the demand."

Lalonda throws her hands up in the air in disgust. "Ugh! You're such a nerd! I don't care how it works, I just want my power!"

I hold my hands up in mock surrender. "Ok, so simply put, everything we need to make it work is at the old power station, and the closer the windmills are, the better it will work."

"Fine! I still want preference when it starts working, though." The evidence of Lalonda's early spoiling grows with each encounter.

I'm trying to respond calmly, but struggling. "I'm sure we can find a way to work it out so everyone benefits from this project."

The bell above the front door jingles as two casually dressed, middle-aged men step inside. I recognize the taller, stocky one as Marshall Stanton, the owner of the scrap yard in Harrison. His time out in the sun this past almost year has given him a dark tan everywhere but where his sunglasses, now tucked into his shirt collar, sit. I quickly stand to greet them.

"Marshall, how are you?" I say, shaking his strong, work-worn hand, just as my father would have done.

"Doing alright, Ray, you?" Marshall asks with a polite smile.

"Doing well, looking forward to our conversation today. You beat the representatives from Carlsburg, but we can chat a bit in the meantime. Who do you have with you today?" I ask.

"This is Adam Kingsley." Marshall places his hand behind Adam's shoulder. Adam is equally tan, but unlike Marshall's graying brown hair and clean-shaven face, Adam's medium blonde hair meets a short, kempt beard over a slender but strong physique.

"He is a particularly helpful fellow who has been working on ways to improve our town and get it ready for the possibility of electricity. I thought his expertise could be helpful to our conversation." Marshall adds, dropping his hand back down to his side.

"Welcome, Adam, I'm glad you made it."

I shake his hand as well. This reminds me of so many times I watched my father make deals with different members of our old community. I so hope he would be proud of me today.

Turning, I gesture to the still-seated hostess. "Gentlemen, I would like to introduce you to Miss Lalonda Pressley. She is the owner of the trucks, I believe we will need for this project, as well as this restaurant. If you are hungry, she has a very talented cook on call."

"We ate before we came, but thank you very much. Miss Lalonda, it is a pleasure to meet you."

Marshall and Adam slide into the booth seat before me, and Marshall offers his hand to Lalonda as well before sliding into the booth seat. She instantly transforms into her more charming self, no doubt a product of years of schmoozing up to rich gentlemen she came across in her past trade.

"The pleasure is all mine, gentlemen. Ray here tells me you have a proposition for me?" Lalonda says somewhat flirtatiously.

Marshall quickly jumps in, "Well, actually, Ray came to us with the idea and we think she very well may be onto something."

Trying to avoid breaking character, Lalonda barely hides her irritation with me. "Yes, well, I'd much rather hear your thoughts on it."

"Sure, should we wait for the rest of the group to arrive?" Marshall frowns lightly, appearing visibly uncomfortable with Lalonda's behavior.

Quickly trying to keep things on track, I reply, "Good idea, Marshall. Perhaps you can tell us a bit about things in your town in the meantime?"

Marshall clears his throat. "I suppose they are a lot like most places, hard. We've been able to keep people from starving, but we don't have nearly the amount of farmland close by as you do, so a lot has to be done through trade. There is a big trading post that has been set up a couple of towns over from us. I'm not sure if you know about it. We had a couple of warehouses survive the fires, so we've been going through and trading what we can from there. It's not going to last forever, though, so we really need to get some other things going." His honesty shows his deep care for his neighbors, an admirable quality.

I nod in response. "I hear you there. I'm glad you've been able to make things work so far. I don't get past our little neck of the woods much, but I have occasionally heard of other places, and most just haven't fared well at all."

The bell above the door sounds again as three more men, also middle-aged and casually dressed, although slightly neater in appearance, enter the front of the restaurant.

"Here comes the rest of our group." I smile and stand to greet them as well.

Andy Dixon, a clean-shaven man with short brown hair and a medium build, the owner of the manufacturing plant in Carlsburg, is the first through the door, and, seeing me, he heads straight toward the corner and the group in the booth.

I greet the men, "Andy, so good to see you again! Who do you have with you today?"

"This here is the sitting mayor of Carlsburg now, James Reed," referring to the tall, slender man with thick-rimmed glasses, light red hair, and a serious look, "and my head engineer, Peter Wallace." Peter is a younger-looking man, still neat in overall appearance, but sporting an untrimmed medium brown beard, under slightly shaggy hair, and carrying a stoic sadness in his eyes.

"Welcome, gentlemen, let me introduce you to the group, then we'll get started." Shaking each man's hand in turn, just as before.

Gesturing back to the table again, "Andy, let me introduce Miss Lalonda Pressley, she is the owner of the trucks I mentioned that may be helpful in transporting everything. This here is Marshall Stanton and Adam Kingsley from Harrison. They represent the scrap yard we hope to use for the majority of the parts needed for the project. They also bring experience working with the parts to the table as we plan out the systems.

Turning to the group already in the booth, I introduce the newcomers in turn.

"May I introduce Andy Dixon, James Reed, and Peter Wallace from Carlsburg, who represent the manufacturing plant where I hope to have the systems assembled?

Gentlemen, won't you have a seat?" Gesturing to the remaining space in the large round booth where we all slide in together.

"Now that we are all here, I'd like to first take the opportunity to thank each of you for considering this proposal for a joint venture, which I hope will serve to greatly benefit each of our communities. I have asked Andy to work up some possible plans for the windmills so we can determine what parts would be necessary. I have also asked Marshall to bring an inventory of what he thinks he has available so we can decide on which set of plans would be the most likely to succeed.

Andy, would you care to start us off?"

Andy's tone is polite but all business as he responds. "Sure, so there are three possibilities we have drawn up based on the general components known to be part of a jet engine and a propeller engine." Andy uncaps a large cardboard tube and starts laying out draft papers on the table for everyone to see.

"The first would be the typical, large-blade vertical style windmill. It is designed to be placed on top of an existing structure, or ideally, a steel power pole. This would save on materials and make it much easier to transport. The biggest drawback is that it would be difficult to get up onto a pole high enough to be effective without finding a functioning crane."

Marshall raises his right hand off the table in front of him and chimes in. "We do have a working crane in the scrapyard, but the fuel to move it far would be tough. We might be able to mount something like that in our town if it came to it, though, I just don't see how we can reasonably get it to the other two towns."

Andy, looking a little surprised, nods his head and replies, "That's really good to know. It definitely affords us more possibilities."

Shifting the papers, Andy continues, "The second option is a much smaller vertical unit that works the same way as the first, but would be mounted on a shorter steel pole. This gives it limited potential height because of the transportation needs, but makes it easier to raise. It would not be as efficient, but it would still be helpful. It could also be made from smaller pieces, so depending on what is available to work with, it may give us just a few more units to add to the overall grid."

Shifting once more, he reveals the third set of plans. "The third option is a horizontal version loosely based on the idea of the vent cap you see on a roof. They could be mounted on top of buildings, or in an open field set up at ground level."

Peter takes over the presentation, pointing out key areas on the plans as he speaks. "These are our favorites for a lot of reasons. With the bearings and blades inside a jet engine, we can heat and bend what is already there into the shape needed, and it would be able to capture wind from any direction, whereas the vertical units can only do this if we add additional moving parts. The problem with that is the more parts it takes, the more that can break, and the faster we use up the available parts as well."

We pass the plans around the table, each taking a moment to consider what we see. Even Lalonda feigns interest here and there.

Looking at the third set of plans for just a moment, I reply, "This all sounds very well thought out. I agree that the horizontal unit sounds the most logical. Marshall, what are we looking at as far as parts? Would that version be the best with what you have available?"

Marshall rubs his chin thoughtfully. "Well, I have 23 scrapped jets in the yard right now. I can't guarantee that all of the pieces you want from the engines are in top shape, but we can check them over before sending them your way, so we start with the best first. Perhaps the damaged ones can be repaired in the meantime. If I can have a copy of your plans, I can have my guys work on repairing what we can."

Peter carefully begins to gather the papers and organize them in front of him as Andy says, "We have a list for you, but we'd like to retain the plans."

Understandably defensive at the implications, Marshall shoots back. "What do you think we're gonna steal your ideas or something? You don't know me, you should definitely not go accusing me of being a thief!"

Andy raises his hands in front of him, "I'm not accusing you of anything, but you're right, I don't know you, and I don't just put everything out there where it can be taken. If you had the plans, what would stop you from cutting us out?" Andy's tone is a combination of honest questioning and slight defensiveness, not yet escalated to match Marshall's.

Before things can spiral further, I interject, "Ok, gentlemen, please! Andy, no one here is going to cut anyone out of anything. We all need each other for this to work the way it is supposed to. That does mean that we all need to extend some trust and also be trustworthy."

Trying to keep the peace, James adds a bit of reason. "Andy, wait, let's see this through, we came all this way because you believed Ray had a good plan, now let's just see where this goes."

Relieved to have an ally, I continue, "Thank you, James. Andy, I hear your concerns, and I don't believe that they are entirely unwarranted. You don't know everyone at this table, and it would be possible for someone to try to cheat or steal from the group. I don't believe that will happen, and I intend to do everything I can to keep it from happening, but I cannot do this alone. Any sort of action we take as a group is still going to take a certain agreement, as far as trust goes, in order for it to work.

Now, perhaps a compromise can be had. Andy, did you make the list of parts you need for each plan that we spoke of?"

"Yes, they're right here." Peter sorts through the papers and pulls out a few sheets of note paper.

"Ok, Marshall, can you and Adam have a look at the list for the horizontal plans and see if you need any details on any of the parts, as you suggested?"

"Yeah, we can do that," Marshall replies, less defensively, but still unhappy.

Realizing she is being left out of the conversation, Lalonda's face betrays her as she scrambles for something to add.

"Wait, who said I was ok with all of this? Were you even going to let me talk, Ray? It is, after all, impossible without *my* trucks."

Expecting something like this to happen doesn't make it any less unwelcome. "Lalonda, do you have any suggestions or questions that we may have missed?" I ask.

"I just want to make the point that without me, none of this happens, so what am I going to get out of it?" Charade melting into entitlement again leaves the men staring at Lalonda instead of reviewing the notes. I continue to try to keep the peace.

"We just talked about this a little while ago, remember? We all benefit from the ability to start harnessing energy to begin to have electricity again."

"I know that, but I want more than just one-third of the windmills, and I want them here." Stubborn arms crossing as she is digging in to try to get her way.

"Hey, without us, you don't even have the parts to make a windmill! If anyone should have a larger share, it should be us!" Marshall points at himself, again defending his position.

"I don't think so! Your parts are sitting there, useless and rusting. Without us, this would never happen either!" Andy adds, his arms crossed and face covered in a stubborn attitude.

My frustration is getting the better of me, and I hear myself sigh heavily. *Why can't we all just do this nicely?*

"Ok, everyone, please! You are all correct, none of this is possible unless we all work together. Since we all have such important roles, we have to be equals, which means equal treatment and equal benefit."

I look across the table pointedly. "Lalonda, again, we already discussed why this can't just be for your personal benefit. The town is providing the fuel for the trucks, so it isn't just your sacrifice to make this happen."

Turning to the side, I work to try to calm the rest of the group leaders, looking at each of them in turn. "Marshall, obviously, this would be next to impossible without your parts, and we greatly appreciate your willingness to work with all of us to provide those items for the greater good.

Andy, your team's engineering abilities and the machinery you have offered to help create these things are indispensable to the cause we are trying to organize and may prove imperative for future projects as well.

I ask each of you to consider this logically: we all need each other, and this partnership has the possibility to do amazing things for all of us. We have to let go of the struggle we seem to be having about who has the most value. That is an incalculable number and doesn't do anyone any good. Can we all agree to this?"

After a moment of silence and a lot of nervous glances around the table, Andy is the first to respond. "Yeah, I see your point. I'll try to keep it in mind."

Relieved, I continue, "Thank you, Andy, truly. Marshall, Lalonda?"

With an exaggerated sigh and rolled eyes, Lalonda adds in, "You know how I feel about it, and that isn't going to change, but I can try to play nice for now."

"I appreciate that, Lalonda. I hope we can work this out as things improve to your satisfaction." Looking over next to Lalonda, I ask, "Marshall, you in?"

Marshall sighs as well, arms crossed, but resigned to work with the situation. "Yeah, I'm in, I just want to be respected, you know?"

I nod in genuine agreement. "Absolutely! We all deserve respect and need to respect each other. I really think this could be the start of something that will make all the difference going forward. Who knows, maybe we can work out other options like solar in the future as well! Can you imagine?"

Marshall chuckles and shakes his head. "You have got to be one of the most optimistic people I've ever met, Ray."

I let loose a slight chuckle. "I doubt that, but I try to see potential where I can anyway.

Ok, so shall we call this a successful meeting and get started on our roles? We can plan to bring a convoy to Harrison one week from today to pick up the plane parts, then take them on to Carlsburg. Can we plan on a minimum of the parts for three systems?"

Marshall looks back at the list on the table. "I think we can do that, this list is pretty extensive, but I have a few guys I can bring in to help."

"Andy, will you be ready to start by then?" I ask, shifting my gaze back over to him.

Andy shrugs, "I'd be ready to start tomorrow, but a week will give us a little more time to optimize things on our end."

"This sounds great. Thank you all for coming. I'll plan on chatting with each of you in one week!"

Chapter Ten

Things That Go Wrong and Things That Go Right

The bell on the door rings yet again, only this time unexpectedly. In walks the Sheriff and his senior deputy, Steven, who is also his right-hand man, followed by two more deputies.

"What's this? A meeting without me? Nah, that can't be it, I know no one would be foolish enough to talk over something important without me. You must all be just here having lunch. Oh wait, there aren't any dishes... interesting." The Sheriff's words come with a menacing tone that sounds anything but safe.

A crashing sound comes from the kitchen where one of the deputies has just entered.

"Oh, there they are! They're in the kitchen. You must have some great waitresses to have cleared the table so completely."

Lalonda is the first to speak. "What are you doing here, Sheriff? I thought you and I had a rendezvous later this afternoon."

I usually don't appreciate Lalonda's slinky flirtations, but right now I really want to get everyone safely out of this room.

"You know, I must have had my times mixed up. Gosh, I'm sorry. Maybe you can include me in what y'all have been talking about while we pass the time before I was supposed to pick you up." He continues to stroll through the maze of tables toward the back corner booth where our group is seated, frozen as he approaches.

The tension in the room only grows thicker as everyone notices the false politeness in the dangerous look on the Sheriff's face. It is clear that he is a man on a mission, and no one wants to tangle with him when he finally breaks this façade to reveal his true intentions.

Attempting to bring calm to the situation, I start to speak. "Sheriff, actually, I'm glad you're here..." Unfazed, he quickly interrupts.

"I bet you are Raylene. I bet you've been waiting for me for a long time. Don't worry, you'll get your turn. There's plenty of the Sheriff to go around. Isn't that right, baby?" A nod towards Lalonda is meant to include her, but only serves to inflame her further.

"Whatever you say, lover."

The look on Lalonda's face is a combination of disappointment and a scathing hatred for me as she turns back towards me just enough to make sure I know she is not at all pleased with being discarded so publicly.

Desperate to free our guests of danger, I try to play along. "These gentlemen were just leaving. Perhaps we can sit down and have lunch, just the three of us."

"You'd like that, wouldn't you?" The Sheriff licks his lips at the thought.

It's baffling how watching a man obviously having impure thoughts about you can make you feel almost as dirty as if you had been undressed for real. As much as I don't want to be in less company with this man, my concern for our guests and furthering our deal is weighing on me heavily.

"Sure, what would you like? I'll go let the cook know." I move to stand up and go towards the kitchen. The Sheriff moves into my path and interrupts my movement.

"The cook isn't available at the moment."

The deputy who had gone into the kitchen and presumably caused the crash of dishes has now come out front to join the rest of us, looking slightly disheveled and quite pleased with himself.

"Why not?" I ask, horrified at the potential answer.

"He's just... busy." The deputy replies with an evil grin splitting his face.

Wanting to check on the cook to see if they need help, I try again. "Ok, why don't I head into the kitchen and I will find something for us to snack on while we wait."

The Sheriff loses his fake calm and shouts back. "No one is going anywhere, don't you get that? You think you are *so* smart, don't you? You think you can scheme behind my back and not get caught? Well, let me inform you of just how mistaken you are."

Before he even finishes his statement, a pistol appears, leveled straight at me. His tone calms, only slightly, as he begins to pressure me back towards the seat.

"Now we are all going to sit, and you are going to include me in your little treachery, then I will decide who can leave. You're all going to pay for treating me this way, I just haven't decided how yet."

"I don't think so, Sheriff."

Those five words are easily the most I've ever heard Bruno say all at once. My surprise is easily forgotten when I turn and realize he and three more of Lalonda's men have appeared through the front door with weapons raised.

Realizing our opportunity, I whisper to the others, "We should leave quickly; we can go out the side door."

Andy quickly rolls up the remaining papers on the table. "Let's do it before this gets any crazier."

"That's the first thing you've said today that I can't argue with, Andy!" Marshall, the furthest into the booth, is happy to have the chance to slide out.

Quickly, we all make it out the door, and while I feel guilty for leaving Lalonda and her men to calm things down, she has a far better chance of it than I do at this point. Hopefully, this will be the last time he interferes like this. He is too unstable to be included, which is why he wasn't invited. *Who could have told him about the meeting?*

Jamal silently joins us as we make our escape through the side door. The Sheriff is also a known racist, and there is nothing good going to come of him being in a room with an already beaten, dark-skinned boy when his temper is already so far gone.

"Gentlemen, I would like to emphatically apologize. We have a complicated hierarchy here. You just met the Sheriff, who honestly needs professional help at this point, but things being what they are, it isn't like we can have him committed. I truly hope things will calm down around him, but I fear one day his end will be violent. I pray it doesn't come to that, but as you witnessed, there is an incredibly dangerous instability about him. I hope we can still be partners despite this uncomfortable occurrence."

Andy reaches his hand out to shake mine. "We understand, Ray. I think we may just need to find a different meeting location should we all need to come together again."

Marshall smiles, "Definitely! Shoot, we're really starting to agree on things. Maybe we'll end up friends after all, Andy."

We all part ways, and I start to walk Jamal back to the house to change his dressings.

"I think the Sheriff has someone else at Miss Lalonda's tellin' 'im stuff."

"Did you hear something, Jamal?" I ask, a quizzical look on my face.

Jamal nods, "I saw one of her guys leave out the side door when everyone started showin' up earlier. He was back outside the window watchin' everythin' when the Sheriff come in."

"Do you know who it was?"

Jamal shakes his head, "I dunno 'is name, but I know he works there."

"Hmm, well, if you see him again, try to find out who he is. It may be important."

"Yes, ma'am."

Walking into the house, Jamal slowly heads to the back room while I start out to the garden for fresh herbs. To my surprise, Lola and Matthew are out weeding the vegetable patch. Both look up as I open the door.

"Oh, hello, Miss Ray. Matthew was goin' on about you teachin' him about weedin' the garden, but not havin' the time to finish it, so we thought we'd come 'roun' and have a go at it to surprise you." Lola smiles up from her crouched position in front of the tomatoes.

"Are you surprised, Auntie?" Asks Matthew.

Such a sweet, thoughtful boy, in some ways anyway. His hurried hug just now has undoubtedly left me with dirty hand prints on my back, and was exactly what I needed after the crazy scene at The Restaurant. I happily hug him back as much as you can hug someone whose head only comes to the middle of your stomach.

"Oh yes, Matthew! This was a great surprise, and you've done an excellent job! I'm very proud of you, and I appreciate all of your hard work. What do you say we take a break and fix something cool to drink?"

Matthew pulls away excitedly. "Ooh! Can I make Miss Lola some strawberry water?"

I bend down to his level with my hands on my knees. "Yes, you certainly can. Do you remember how to pick the sweet ones?"

"Sure I do!" Matthew turns to look at Lola. "Miss Lola, can I fix you some strawberry water?"

Lola smiles widely at such a kind thought. "Well, I'd love that. Let's get washed up 'fore we go in the house though."

I start to walk over to the herb portion of the garden. "Jamal is with me, I'm just going to get some more herbs for his wrap. I'll be ready in a bit."

Finishing up with Jamal, I decide to leave him to rest in the back room. Poor boy is still in a lot of pain. The herbs are helping, but time and God's amazing systems in the body will be the real healers.

"Here, Auntie Ray, I made you some strawberry water too." Matthew hands me a small glass of water with a sliced strawberry floating in it.

"Thanks, bud! It looks yummy."

I take a drink and, tipping the glass down, I see Matthew with a worried look on his face. "Is Jamal going to be ok? We heard him while you were fixing him, and it didn't sound very good."

It never fails to amaze me just how in tune this young child is with what goes on around him. I so hope that it doesn't change him to see so much darkness in the world.

I reach over and rub his little back. "He'll be just fine, it'll just take him a little while to feel better."

His look lightens just a bit with the idea of good news. "That's good, I miss playing catch with him."

I squeeze his shoulder into me in a side hug. "I know you do. I'm sure he misses it too. Say, why don't you make him a glass of this yummy water and take it to him?"

"Alright! I can do that."

Matthew quickly runs out the back door to find a few more strawberries.

"He's such a good boy. You're doin' a good job with him." Lola washes another glass and fills it with clean water for Jamal.

I sit down on one of the stools in the kitchen. "I wish I could spend more time with him, though. He is so special, and he has lost so much, I don't know how I could even start to make it up to him." I stare at the glass in front of me, suddenly lost in thought.

"Nah, he loves you, an' he's happy. Life may look off from the way it was 'posed to go, but it's still good." Lola snaps me out of it with a sweetness all her own.

"Thanks, Lola. I really appreciate all you and Mama Lou do for him. Lord knows I couldn't manage without you!" I smile at her, truly thankful for her kindness.

"Lord knows you're doin' important work. You have a callin', Miss Ray, and if us watchin' that sweet boy helps, then I'd say we have a callin' too."

Matthew has already delivered his gift to Jamal and comes bouncing back into the room.

"Jamal liked my water, Auntie Ray."

He quickly climbs up on my lap for a hug. How big he has become and how much he reminds me of Cameron. So many thoughts and feelings all flash through me in the moment it takes him to snuggle in. Maybe this is what it would feel like to have a child of my own.

"Of course, he liked it, you make the best strawberry water anywhere."

"You really think so?"

He pulls away to look me in the face with one hand on each of my cheeks. The excited expectancy on his face makes my heart melt. Oh, how I wish we could all be so innocent and easy to please.

"Absolutely!"

I snuggle him in again. So many more feelings. If only all of the pain and craziness outside these walls could never make it inside and touch these beautiful moments. A silent resolution to fight for these times for all of the families, not just my own, forms in my heart. Change is coming.

Chapter Eleven

That's the Truth

Another day, and this one brings a need to work out some pretty huge problems with two very different groups. The fake soldiers have been waiting at the hotel outside of town, supposedly anyway, for a couple of days now, and are certain not to remain patient long. There still doesn't seem to be a simple solution for that situation, so it will have to wait. Right now, I hope to have an appointment with the leaders of the homeless kids. I've set up waiting in the alley next to The Restaurant with some fresh produce and cheese from one of the farms, just in case they agree to meet with me.

"Hey, you, Miss Ray?" A voice calls out of the shadows just out of sight. I turn towards the sound.

"I am, may I ask your name?"

A few shapes move closer towards me.

"You can call me Boss."

"Alright, Boss, and who do you have with you?"

His defensive posture, still standing back several feet from me, arms crossed and head up, trying to look bigger than he is, although he is not at all small, makes it clear he did not come here to be messed with.

"You don't need to be asking questions. We're just here to figure you out."

I raise my hands in mock surrender. "Fair enough. I appreciate you taking the time to meet with me. I had a few thoughts that might help your community, and I do recognize that it is your community, so out of respect for your position, I wanted to discuss them with you to see if we can work out a deal."

"Isabelle told me what you had talked about; I'll listen, but no promises." His face softens ever so slightly, obviously not prepared to be treated with respect.

"If Isabelle told you about our conversation, then I won't waste your time having it again. Since I wasn't there when you spoke, I'm happy to clear up anything that wasn't communicated well or answer any questions you may have. Would you like more details?"

"Look, we don't need anybody's charity. We can take care of ourselves." More of the bravado, but also determination, is likely the cause of their survival to date.

"Yes, you can, you have been doing a remarkable job of it. I am simply proposing a possible upgrade to your abilities where you would still, in large part, manage things, you would just have the support of the rest of the community."

Surprised and a little confused, Boss asks, "So you're not trying to take over and do the typical adult control freak thing then?"

I shake my head. "No, I don't want to, nor do I have time to run this. I would be more of what you might consider a board member. I can help make decisions and deals to make things work well, but the day-to-day stuff would not be up to me. There would be other adults involved as well, but we would be counting on you, young men, to continue to do the majority of the care and management of those younger than you.”

Boss remains defensive, arms still crossed, but the scowl he has been sporting is beginning to lessen. “How do we know we can trust you to do what you’re saying? Maybe you just want to find out where we’ve been living so you can take what we have for yourself.”

“I suppose the only way you can truly know if you can trust me is if you give me the chance to earn it. Would you take a walk with me?” I say, motioning behind him down the alley towards the school.

“Where are we going?”

“The high school a few blocks south. No tricks, I promise. It’s a big part of my idea,” I respond.

Boss takes a brief pause before agreeing. “Yeah, I guess we can do that. You pull anything I don’t like, though, and things are gonna get ugly fast.” His point was accentuated with a pointed finger in my direction.

“Fair enough. Do you guys want to grab these bags here? I brought some more produce and some fresh cheese from one of the local farms I work with. I know the mats and this bit of food aren’t enough to solve the problems you guys are facing. I hope together we can change that.”

The boys pick up the bags, looking inside. Boss looks back at me, with a sincerity in his voice, he says, “Thank you for the food. That does help.”

While walking to the school with these boys, the tension they arrived with is beginning to fade. Turns out Boss’ name is Justin Turner. The two boys with him are his cousins, Cole and Brady Miller. Although they are cousins, they bear such a similar resemblance that they could have been brothers. Each of the boys has shaggy, light brown hair that is long and in need of a cut. Their teenage stubble has gone without the benefit of a razor and has created thin, scrubby beards on each of their faces. Their youthful strength and the lack of food has left their average frames lean, but still athletic. Their clothes are both worn and a bit dirty, and they each smell as though they have not had access to much water.

They were all at school during the coming and when they finally made it to their homes, all of their parents were among the disappeared, so they stuck together and found several other students, who has been growing in the months since.

We arrive at the school grounds to find quite a mess. The neglect, paired with the damage done by angry, scared, and unsupervised children, has taken a toll. The buildings are still largely intact, and the possibilities are still great.

Coming up to the front of the main building, I start to show them what I am picturing as we look around, knowing they would have attended this school and would be familiar with it. "So I know the school is pretty rough right now, but what if we could clean up the grounds, put in some gardens, and repurpose the classrooms to make a place for sleeping? We can look at setting the cafeteria back up, and keep a few rooms for classes, not the same as before, but vocational things that can be useful for survival and for the community, including apprenticeships and things that are needed to make things better.

If you're open to it, there are a few other children in the area who have been staying with friends and family who might also come in during the day for some of the classes, but they would not be taking resources. If anything, they would be adding to the hands to help with things like growing food here."

"Do you really have people who want to do this, though? Why would anyone want to do all this for a bunch of other people's kids?" Cole asks looking a bit confused and unsure.

"I've approached a few people, but I wanted to know what your thoughts were before I went too far. There are still a lot of people in the community who know things that could really help."

"So you're saying we still get to be in charge and we can have the whole place, plus you'll help us find food, work, and the things we need to be comfortable. What do you get out of it? There has to be something; nobody does anything this crazy without asking for something back."

I respect Justin's instincts, even if he is questioning everything I say. He is already learning to be a good leader, in part because of the caution he exercises. Winning him over will be a great benefit to everyone involved.

"I am not sure I have an answer you will believe, but the truth is that I care very deeply for people. I believe in Yeshua the Messiah, and the Bible says that every person has value. It is important for each of us to do what we can to care for those around us and make the world a better place. If the things I have in mind help even one of you, it will have been worth it to me. That's the truth. If you need another reason, every person who contributes and helps those around them makes things better for everyone else. If I help you and you help someone else, it is good for everyone. Does that make sense?"

Justin pauses again, wanting to believe me, but still cautious. "We'll have to talk about it, and we'll let you know. I'll send the Embry children when we've made a decision."

"Thank you all very much for considering this. If you have any other questions or thoughts, please send word. I'll wait for your decision."

Chapter Twelve

Challenging the Crazy

Heading home from the high school feels like more of a trudge than a walk. While I should feel hopeful and start planning out who to talk to about turning this idea into reality, I am overwhelmed with the weight of how to best handle the soldiers. I need to take care of this before they come back into town in an even less cooperative mood than before.

Arriving home, I find Franklin and Isabelle on my back porch.

"Well, hi guys, how are you?" I offer a little wave as I come around the corner.

"Hi Miss Ray, how did the meet up go with Boss?" Isabelle asks.

"I think it went pretty well, considering. They are supposed to discuss it, then send you two to let me know what they decide."

Isabelle's eyes go wide. "You didn't tell them we knew where you lived, did you?"

"No, it didn't come up at all. Are you hungry?" I ask as I lead them inside.

"We're ok, thank you," Isabelle answers again. Franklin's face doesn't agree, but I decide not to push too hard.

"Well, if you'd like to take anything with you, let me know. I'm a little light since I sent a bunch with the boys earlier, but there are still a few things out there."

It's strange how a sound can instantly change everything about a moment. You can be totally peaceful and calm, then suddenly the world closes in as the telltale sounds of trouble approach. Today, that sound came in the form of four large diesel engines. The soldiers are coming back, and there is little doubt that this will be an unpleasant happening.

"Miss Ray, what is that?" Isabelle's worry is evident with the noisy intrusion. My own face has grown instantly grim at the sound as well. I try to correct and put up a quick smile to reassure the children.

"If I'm not mistaken, it is the sound of a few large engines bringing some rather unpleasant people for a visit. You guys should probably head out. I'm not sure these men have polite intentions in coming here."

Franklin goes to the window to try to see what's coming.

"Were they in town before? They're all military-type vehicles, right?" Franklin says, still trying to catch a glimpse down the street.

"Yes, what do you know of it?" I ask.

Without taking his eyes off the view down the street, Franklin replies. "We saw lights going past the place we've been staying a few days ago, and I went outside to see what it was."

Isabelle's eyes go wide. "Franklin, you didn't!"

"I wanted to see. What if it was our parents? Nobody saw me. It's totally okay." Franklin turns around and looks at the floor, now dejected from his sister's scolding.

"Can you tell me about where this is? I think they came up from the post south of town, but I'm not positive. No one reported seeing them come into town before they showed up here in front of my house a couple of days ago."

The children look at each other as if silently asking whether they should say something or not. Isabelle nods yes to Franklin.

"It's outside of town off of South 80, so they could have come up from the post," Franklin says carefully.

"Ok, thank you both. You really should go before they get here. I really appreciate your help. Stay safe, ok?" I say hurriedly, concerned for their safety should they be caught here.

"You too, Miss Ray. Come on, Franklin." Isabelle hurries Franklin out the back door, and they are gone quickly.

There is no mistaking that they are close now, the rank smell of diesel exhaust fills the air through the open windows as the engines bring the men closer. Time to face them, whether I like it or not, but not until everyone in the house is safe. Lola and Matthew were waiting for me to get back, and have just come in the door. Jamal is resting in the back room as well.

"Matthew, can you please go in and see how Jamal is doing? Maybe take your trucks in with you." I suggest with as calm a face as I can muster.

Gently, I pull Lola aside so I can whisper to her privately. No need to worry, Matthew, if I can avoid it.

"There is a pistol on the top shelf in the closet in Jamal's room. It is loaded; all you need to do is push the safety on the left side down so you can see the red mark on the side, aim it, and squeeze the trigger, only if you need to. I don't think you will, but just in case."

"Oh, I hope it doesn't come to that. Surely it can't…"

The realization of exactly what I'm saying hits her, and admirably, she stands a little taller, as if her resolve to protect those boys fills her body, pushing it up past its normal height.

"I'll do what I gotta."

BAM BAM BAM

"Open up, Ray, we're tired of waiting on you."

Lola quickly moves into the back room and closes the door. I take one more second and a very deep breath to help calm my pounding heart just a bit before opening the door to what promises to be a difficult situation.

"Captain, I wasn't expecting you. Perhaps we should speak outside." I move to walk out into the yard, but am quickly blocked by the Captain.

"Oh no, now that I know about your little army of neighbors, I think we should speak inside."

As if this were his home instead of mine, he pushes past me right into the living room before turning to face me again. Hopefully, I can keep him from going any further.

"Ok, we can speak inside then. I was actually preparing to come out to see you, so thank you for saving me the trip," I say with as much politeness as I can muster.

"Spare me your pleasantries, we have waited on you for days. We could have been to several more towns instead of sitting on our thumbs at that crummy motel." The Captain's tone is exactly how I would expect, loud, harsh, and threatening.

"I can understand your frustration, and I sincerely apologize for my part in it. Things here are complicated, and it is difficult for me to get away from the chaos most days."

"I didn't come here for your excuses, I need supplies and men, now are you going to give them to me or not?"

I take another deep breath, both to calm myself and to stall just a second longer.

"The short answer is no. Frankly, we don't have resources to spare for anyone who doesn't contribute to our community, and I am not going to ask the diminished number of men who are still here to sacrifice themselves to a cause they don't believe in. I do have a counterproposal for you and your men, though. I'd like to present it to all of you together. Since we both know you aren't actually soldiers, it seems reasonable that they should be able to make their own decisions," I say while gesturing toward the door, and the men out in the yard beyond.

The Captain counters with a pointed finger and narrowed eyes. "Not so fast. You're a sneaky one, aren't you? I am still the one in charge. You can speak to me first, and I'll decide if we should go to them or not."

The obvious anger and aggression exhibited by his demeanor remind me of a bully I used to see at school as a teen. He always postured boldly with his chest out and chin up when his ill-intended ideas were building. It was a definite warning to be sure.

"I'm certainly not trying to be sneaky, I am simply a cautious person. Perhaps the wisdom in that can serve to make us allies in this crazy world. While I can't say that I agree with leaving your men outside, I will respect your wishes on this for the sake of recompense for keeping you waiting. That chaos I mentioned earlier is as much a domestic threat as it is foreign. There is a leader of a part of town who is frankly a bit insane. Things being what they are, he is not receiving the help he needs, and grows more dangerous by the day."

"You must be insane! Why on earth would we give up our mission to squash a stupid disagreement you have with some guy?" The Captain waves his arms in frustration, beginning to pace in the small space of the living room.

"Frankly, we could really use your help. I have worked very hard to help rebuild our community, which makes us a target for outsiders, and when you factor in the self-sabotage we face from the inside, things here are looking to escalate and destroy so much of the progress that has been made. I would like to offer you and your men a position here. You need supplies. We can always benefit from more protection. We can provide you with living quarters, food, clothes, etc., and you wouldn't need to stay on the road looking for those things. If you decide you really want to go fight in the outlands, we are very close and it would give you a place to stage from when you are ready, although I would ask that you approach them from a ways away so they don't come here to retaliate should you be unsuccessful. Basically, I want to hire you to protect our town."

The Captain runs his hand down over his face in disbelief and anger. "No, our demands stand as they are. Either give us the supplies and men to fight, or we will take them. Maybe I'll start here."

The Captain advances towards me as I have backed towards the back door to create space, when I notice he is becoming more agitated. He doesn't know that I carry a well-used 9mm pistol with me, a gift from my brother on my 16th birthday. It may be down to its last three bullets, but you can't tell that from the outside. I expertly draw the familiar piece of metal and aim it at his face since he has wisely chosen to wear body armor today.

"I'm afraid I can't let you do that."

He stops and shakes his head, hands on his hips.

"I knew you were hiding something."

He puts his right hand up pointing at me, eyes narrowed into slits.

"This isn't over, not by a long shot. You'll regret the way you've treated me; just wait."

The sneer left on his face reminds me of the Sheriff in that moment. Perhaps he wouldn't have been helpful after all. The front door slams as he walks out to the vehicles waiting in the street. In a puff of exhaust, they are gone as quickly as they came.

One thing is certain: this isn't over, and it just became much more difficult.

Chapter Thirteen

Taking a Trip

Today is the first trip to transfer parts from Harrison to Carlsburg with Lalonda's trucks, and I can't help but worry that something is going to happen. The Sheriff is still angry that we didn't include him in the planning meeting, and no one knows where the soldiers went. I would love to think that they have left town to try someone with less fight in them, but I doubt they will give up so easily.

Surprisingly, Lalonda's trucks are all ready and waiting when I arrive at The Restaurant. I half expected her to change her mind or at least give me an earful before we can pull out, but she is nowhere to be found.

The trip to Harrison is uneventful, almost giving me a sense of security as if maybe I was wrong and nothing is going to happen after all. Pulling into the scrap yard, Marshall meets us and directs us to a large pile of parts. It's a good thing these trucks are capable of carrying two tons each, and we brought three of them with us. Even with those abilities, these trucks still have their work cut out for them. A few people I don't recognize come out and start to help load up the trucks.

That help should have been appreciated, but instead, a couple of Lalonda's men start harassing a couple of the women struggling to lift a large piece of fuselage from the pile. Before I can address it, Bruno steps in and violently shoves both of the men into the side of one of the trucks with a force I would hate to be in front of.

"Apologize," Bruno growls.

One speaks for both, mostly because the other seems too petrified to move.

"We're sorry." He manages to squeak out.

Bruno's eyes narrow, and his grip tightens.

"Better."

This simple command leaves no question that the consequences of disobedience would be brutal.

After a gulp large enough to hear over the 12 feet between us, the man tries again. "We're sorry for our comments." He glances quickly back and forth between Bruno and the women as he speaks, as if making sure he is doing what Bruno wants with each word.

"Please a-a-accept our apologies. Can we help you pick up that piece and load it onto the truck?"

Bruno eases his grip on the men but retains the deadly look on his face.

"Behave."

"Sorry, Bruno."

The intimidating giant of a man who rarely speaks obviously carries much more depth and integrity than I originally recognized, but how could such a seemingly principled man tolerate being surrounded by the corruption and despicable actions coming from Lalonda and these men on a daily basis?

"I'd hate to be those guys, huh?" Marshall says, silently appearing behind me.

I jump just a bit and turn to see who spoke. "Oh! Marshall, you startled me. I agree. I don't know much about him other than he is incredibly reserved and is almost never far away from Lalonda. In fact, I'm surprised he came along, but I'm glad he did. I hope that's all we need him for, but I just have a funny feeling today that something isn't quite right. Hopefully, I'm wrong, but if I had to choose a team, he would certainly be on it."

Concern etches Marshall's brow. "Do you think you need extra help? We have a couple of cars running. I can send them with a few people as an escort if you think it will help."

"I think we'll be ok, but I do appreciate it. Plus, if either of the groups I'm thinking of do come after us, it is all stuff from our town, and I would feel terrible if one of your people was caught up in it."

"As long as you're sure. It doesn't do any of us any good to have this stuff hijacked, you know." Marshall's warranted concern fills his face.

"Believe me, I know. I'll do everything I can to make sure that doesn't happen, you have my word." I offer my right hand to solidify the resolve in my features.

Marshall gives a sideways grin and reaches out his hand to shake mine.

"I'll take it. Let's get you guys on the road, then, huh?"

"Oh, I have a gift!" Moving to the back of the lead truck, I pull out a wooden crate.

"A group that lives outside of town had a good apple season start-up, and they actually had to thin the trees some. I've been helping them with a few ideas, so they left me some. I thought a gift as part of my sincerest apologies for the situation last week might be nice, so I brought a crate of them for you and your people. I hope you enjoy them."

Marshall reaches out to take the crate. "These look amazing! I'm sure we will. Please be sure to extend our thanks."

"Will do!"

Knowing that the guys would probably be unhappy to watch some of the apples they loaded disappear before we started out, I had brought three crates, one for each town's team. Given the looks being flashed around among Lalonda's men, it might be time to get their crate out.

The last of the pieces have been loaded on the trucks, so I walk around with the crate so everyone can grab one or two. The looks on these grown men's faces are reminiscent of days when even these calloused, worldly men were children given a gift of something special and exciting. It's good to be reminded that deep down there is a little something good in each of us, even when the outside hides it away.

Leaving the scrapyard, I'm in the lead truck with Bruno and a man named Jim, whom I hadn't met before, but he seems nice enough. The weather is pleasant, and with the windows down, things just seem to be going well. I feel as though I can relax, peaceful even. It's rare to have these moments when so much is going wrong in the world. I close my eyes and let my hand fall out into the air, rushing by. It's so smooth and cool on my skin. My neck relaxes and my head drifts back onto the headrest, for a moment anyway.

The quiet is interrupted by our driver. "There's a truck off the road ahead."

"Wait, what?" My eyes pop open to see what he is referring to.

"Slow down," Bruno adds in.

The moment is gone. The worry of impending trouble and all of the weight that goes with it slams back into me like a punch in the stomach. Looking closer at the truck, it looks like it has recently been ambushed. There are fresh bullet holes all across the windshield and along the driver's side door. It is mostly off in the ditch on our side, even though it is facing us. It also looks like it had been set on fire afterwards. It's far enough out of the way that we can easily go past it, but something just doesn't feel right. *I hope that was all done while it was empty.*

"Stop short and let's check it out." Says Bruno with his typical unreadable face as he pulls out a pistol, and checks it for rounds before doing the same with the rifle mounted in the window behind him. "I'll go."

I pull out my pistol and check it as well. "Thanks, Bruno, I'm going too. Jim, why don't you stay here just in case the truck needs to move quickly?" I roll my shoulders, steeling myself for whatever we may find here as the truck slows to a stop.

Jumping down from the cab, I don't have the chance to move forward before a shot rings out, ricocheting off the pavement just inches from me.

The shooter loudly orders, "STAY WHERE YOU ARE, AND THROW OUT ANY WEAPONS YOU'RE CARRYING RIGHT NOW!"

My mind is racing. Who could this be? The clothes and weapons don't look like anything the soldiers would have had, and they didn't know anything about this project, so how would they have known to wait for us here? No, it had to be the Sheriff. He was angry we didn't include him in the meeting. That must have been why Lalonda didn't bother with me this morning.

"STEVEN, LET'S TALK," I shout around the edge of the truck door I am hiding behind.

Bruno looks at me from inside the cab like I'm crazy. The only faces we can see all have masks covering them. I'm certain this is the Sheriff's doing, though, which means Steven must be there since he wouldn't trust just anyone to do this kind of work.

"I KNOW IT'S YOU AND THE OTHER DEPUTIES, LET'S TALK. I'M PUTTING DOWN MY WEAPON AND COMING OUT. PLEASE DO THE SAME. THIS DOESN'T HAVE TO BE ANY UGLIER THAN IT ALREADY IS."

I show my pistol out to the side, pointed up and away from the truck, before slowly setting it on the ground. Then, with my hands up, I walk out into the open. I know Bruno still has his weapons up in the cab if the need should arise, and I am again thankful he's on my side, at least for today.

One of the men starts walking out from behind the truck, leaving his rifle on the hood as he passes and comes to meet me in the middle. He lifts his mask and reveals that he is indeed Steven.

"How did you know?" Disbelief and surprise crossed his face.

I lower my hands.

"Who else would know to wait for us on this road and be angry enough to cause trouble besides your boss?"

Steven pinches the bridge of his nose.

"You've got me there. The problem is he's got me where I live, ya know? I have to do what he says."

I nod my head in understanding.

"What exactly are you supposed to be doing here?"

Steven gestures behind me.

"He wants the trucks."

My arms cross, and I take a moment to think.

"Ok, what if we deliver the parts and then let you have them?"

Steven shakes his head.

"He wants everything. He said no one gets to scheme behind his back and get away with it. Lalonda tried to tell him this would help him, too, but he wouldn't listen. They had a big fight after you guys left, and it didn't sound good."

"Is she ok?" I ask, still concerned for her safety, regardless of her behavior.

Steven looks down, sad and almost shameful as he quietly replies, "I'm not sure, he sent us all out beforehand. I wouldn't put it past him to do something bad, though."

My arms uncross, and my hands find my hips as resolve to do the right thing solidifies in my heart, certain that the evil in the world has to be defeated by people standing up against such things.

"Well, we'll have to figure that out once we get back. I hear you on the concerns about things at home. You have family, don't you? I can see why you have so much to fight for. That's exactly what I'm trying to do here. I'm fighting for all of us, and I could really use your help. What is an excuse he would believe? Maybe you missed us, you waited for hours, but we never passed."

Steven looks down and shakes his head again before rising again and finding my eyes.

"I can't take that risk. You just need to get everyone out of the trucks." His tone is almost pleading, not so much with me to do what needs to happen but for the current situation to be over.

I take a couple more steps toward Steven, hoping to close the gap emotionally as well as physically. "Steven, it doesn't have to be this way. You're a reasonable man, what do you think we can do?"

Now agitated, he turns and begins to pace away, then back towards me, half shouting as he comes back, pointing first at himself, then the trucks.

"It's not up to me to think, it's up to me to do, and I am telling you to get out of the trucks! Please don't make me get violent. A peaceful exchange is all that I can offer."

I look down and gently shake my head. "I wish that was the case. I hate to do this, but we have you greatly outnumbered. There is at least one weapon aimed at you right now, just in case things couldn't be solved reasonably. I respect you and your position, and I'm sorry, but I can't let you take these trucks - I won't."

Steven looks at me, half shocked, and completely emotionally weakened by my response.

"You realize you'll be the first one shot if this happens."

I nod, never breaking away from Steven's eyes.

"If that's how it is, then so be it. This is too important to let one person stand in the way."

Disbelief covers his face again as if he were looking at something completely foreign to him.

"You really mean that, don't you? I knew you were different, but that's just plain nuts! You don't mean it." He says questioningly.

"I really do. We have to fight harder than ever to make this world decent again. There is so much suffering, and the only way it will change - the only way for good to triumph is for good people to do something about it! Join us! Help us! Make a difference for your community and your family. Help me make this place somewhere your kids will be happy to come up in." I plead.

Steven pauses, brow furrowed in thought.

"Do you really believe that is possible?"

"I do if we all work together. What do you say? Tell him the truth, you were way outgunned and had no choice but to let us pass. Ask your men, I doubt they want to go through a firefight either."

Another pause, and a sigh, "I hope you're right, Ray."

He points at my face to emphasize his point.

"You better keep your word on all this."

A glimmer of a smile crosses my face, just as a flash of hope runs through my chest. "I promise I will do everything I can to make things better for all of us... everything."

Steven turns back and starts walking to the burned truck. He collects his rifle on the way around to the other side, where the men are waiting.

"Alright, guys, let them go. I'll deal with the Sheriff when we get back."

Nobody moves, completely thrown off guard by the change in orders. Steven strengthens his authority with a sterner tone.

"You all got that? Any questions?"

Heads shake across the group.

"Good, load up then."

Walking back to the open truck, I bend to retrieve my pistol and return it to the familiar place tucked into the holster in the back of my jeans.

Bruno shakes his head at me, shifting over so I can climb back into the cab.

"You're crazy."

"I've been hearing that a lot lately, Bruno, but you know what, if crazy is what it takes, then I must be doing something right."

Climbing back up into the truck had taken a lot more effort than it should have. Trying to hide the fact that every bit of me was shaking from the experience is not an easy task. I think Bruno notices me clutching my hands together, but he doesn't say so. I hope I'm right about him being a good man. I'm still not sure I can afford to show weakness in front of any of these men, regardless of which side they seem to be on at the moment.

*****

"I was beginning to think you changed your mind."

Climbing down from the truck was a bit easier than it had been to climb up just a few minutes before; thankfully, the shaking had subsided in the handful of miles remaining til we arrived at the manufacturing plant.

"Sorry about that, Andy."

I greet him with a handshake, "A couple of things took a little longer than we expected. We have a whole lot of pieces here for you, though. Where would you like them?"

"If you can pull around to the loading dock, I have some people there to help unload." Andy points around the side of the building.

"Perfect! Maybe while they unload, we can chat for a bit."

Jim drives the truck around to the loading dock, followed by the other vehicles. Just as Andy said, a few people came out immediately and started removing the tie-downs from the loads.

Andy and I follow the trucks past the loading area into the main workshop. We stop at a large work table where the plans are all spread out, ready to be implemented. Both of us lean over to study them as we talk.

"If you brought everything on the list, we should be done with the three units in about two weeks. If there is anything missing or dysfunctional, we will need a bit more time. I can send someone to let you know when they are ready to be picked up, though, so you don't have to spend gas going back and forth unnecessarily."

I stand back up straight. "I appreciate that. I like what you have planned so far. I have a couple of guys who used to work for the electric company, trying to work up a storage option and a mounting pad for this. Hopefully, they'll be ready in time."

"Well, take them these." Andy hands me a few pages of detailed schematic drawings.

"It is a set of plans for the wiring, and we have developed some ideas for limiting the power flow so it can be concentrated in smaller areas until more units can be added. It will help to have experienced people do some of the groundwork now. I have a couple of people in a small team that have agreed to go to the other sites to help install everything the first time and get it going, and this will save them a lot of time, provided it is done correctly."

"Absolutely, that makes plenty of sense. I'll be sure to get these to the right people as soon as I can.

Oh! I have a gift for your people as well. There is a crate of apples in the back of one of the trucks as a bit of a thank you. We are very grateful for your help in all of this," I say with a smile.

"You made it happen, I'm glad you thought of us as well. I also hope this will be the start of several such deals, especially if fresh fruit is part of the package!" Andy smiles back. The positive interaction is welcome after our unexpected stop earlier.

Unloading the trucks was a quick job with the help of the workers in the plant, and the trip home was thankfully much less eventful. As we pull up to The Restaurant, the Sheriff's car is parked right out front. Against my better judgment, I go in with the men so I can check on Lalonda. Steven's account of the morning had left me concerned for her. Surprisingly, she and the Sheriff are snuggled in her corner booth quite intimately, and she appears to be well. He looks up at me with a smug look as if somehow he had won something over me, as he puts his arm around her.

"There you are, Ray. I trust everything went well today?"

I put up a fake smile. "Yes, it did, Sheriff. I was just returning the trucks as promised. They worked perfectly, Lalonda, thank you."

Lalonda waves her hand dismissively. "Yeah, whatever. When are you supposed to need them again to go get my windmill?"

"Andy is going to send someone when they are finished, so we don't waste fuel going there to check, but I expect it will be about two weeks," I reply, as politely as I can in such company.

"Well, that's nice of them. You won't need to worry about it, though. Me and my boys are going to handle the transportation now. After all, this sort of thing is man's work, and you never know what sort of trouble you could run into out on the road."

The smirk on the Sheriff's face screams of his deliberate plans to set up that ambush. If only his conniving mind could be put to better use, finding unique ways to fix things instead of making them worse.

"That is very generous of you, but I'd hate to take up your valuable time fussing with something like that."

The Sheriff quickly removes his arm from around Lalonda and sits forward with his elbows on the table.

"Oh, well, see the windmill is coming to me, so it makes more sense for me to manage it."

As much as I don't want to have this conversation, I don't want to foster false expectations either.

"I'm afraid that may not be the best idea. Your part of town doesn't have good access to a main power junction, which is necessary to manage the energy. It makes far more sense to continue with the original plan. You will still receive power once enough can be harvested to power the town, just like everyone else." The tension in the room is building, and I am left feeling a need to retreat, but fighting it instead.

"Well, now see, had you included me in your mutinous little meeting, I would be getting my own, so since you didn't, I'm just going to take yours."

That dangerous look was back again. Will there ever be a simple conversation with this man?

"You weren't included simply because you are part of the same infrastructure as we are, but didn't have anything specifically necessary for this to work, is all. Perhaps it was an oversight, I just didn't want to waste your time," I say, attempting to placate his growing attitude.

The Sheriff scoffs and sarcastically replies, "Waste my time? Oh, how thoughtful of you... Not!"

With the speed of a much more sober man, he is up and moving towards me with his hand back as if he plans to hit me.

"You are a filthy little liar, and someone needs to teach you a lesson!" He shouts.

Before I can navigate the maze of tables and chairs, he has me by the arms with a grip I'd expect more from a machine than a man.

"You just wanted to make me jealous! I know you want me, you've always wanted me." The Sheriff says almost seductively.

Lalonda's face hardens as she realizes his desire for me instead of her. Finding my footing, I lean away from his alcohol-saturated breath as he pokes me hard below my collarbone.

"Don't you worry, you'll get what's coming to you. I always get what I want."

He licks his chapped lips as he begins to look me over. His grip on my arms begins to loosen ever so slightly. Lalonda is behind him, and two slender hands slide between us as she tries to pull his attention back to her. Finally letting go of my arms, he pushes her aside and walks outside.

"See what you've done, now he's gone. Why can't you just leave us alone?" Hugging her arms to her sides, she slowly walks back to her booth. This is one of those moments when my heart just hurts for her. *It must be very empty to live the way she does.*

Chapter Fourteen

It's All in the Details

After the long day, it feels like forever to make 1.5 mile trip to my door. Sitting in the swing on the front porch is the ever-surprising Joshua. He stands as we approach, holding a book I don't recognize and the last bits of an apple from the fourth and last crate on the porch.

As soon as Joshua sees Jamal and I walking back from the Restaurant, he sets his book and apple down.

"Let me help you to bed, Jamal," Joshua says compassionately as he jumps up and slides in under Jamal's right arm, taking the weight I've been bearing from the left. I glance over just in time to catch a wink before they make their way to the back room. *Why does that make me feel so odd?*

Changing Jamal's wrap is so much easier with help, and much less painful for Jamal. It's nice to have an extra pair of hands. Maybe I should get Lola to come over in the evenings more often. I hand Jamal a clean apple and a big cup of herbal tea. It shouldn't be too much longer before he is able to manage without the help. I'm sure that if we had the ability to take X-rays, they would reveal several broken ribs. Undoubtedly, there is plenty of internal tissue damage as well. Thankfully, he doesn't appear to have had any massive bleeding, just lots and lots of bruises.

Leaving Jamal to rest, we go out into the living room where I collapse into my favorite chair, eyes closed, exhausted from the day. Remembering my manners, my eyes pop back open, and I start to sit up.

"Oh, I'm sorry, Joshua, can I get you anything?"

"Long day, huh? Don't worry about me, can I get you some water, or tea?"

I pause for just a moment, considering the offer and its source. He has already started heading for the kitchen before I can even respond.

"You know, tea would be great actually. There should be a jar of sun tea on the counter by the stove. Thank you. And thank you for the apples; they helped make a good impression on the people I'm trying to deal with, as well as several people around here. It was very generous to be sure."

"You're welcome." Joshua smiles widely as he efficiently works through pouring two glasses of the brown liquid. He seems so at home in the kitchen.

"So, how did everything go today?" He asks, handing me one of the glasses.

"Good, then bad, then good, then bad again. The Sheriff has decided he wants to control everything. He sent a bunch of his goons to ambush us on the way to Carlsburg when the trucks were loaded. One of them took a potshot rather near me. It took a lot to talk them down so we could pass. It was all I could do to climb back into the truck afterwards."

"Are you serious?" Joshua sits forward on the loveseat, almost as if ready to spring into action.

"Who shot at you?" The obvious concern in his voice is endearing.

"It's not important; they missed it on purpose, but it was still jarring. I'm hopeful that we actually made some allies today, if that's possible. We are going to need all the help we can get if the Sheriff keeps getting worse. He came after me tonight when we dropped off the trucks. I think he has it in his head that I am in love with him or something."

Why is it so easy to be open with him?

"Are you ok? He didn't hurt you, did he?" His concern is now mixed with controlled anger as he kneels down in front of me.

"Nothing serious, maybe a couple bruises, but they'll heal," I say quietly, looking down at him.

"Please show me, they may need tending."

Even with the anger he is experiencing, there is a softness about him. I can tell he is upset, but he is also gentle.

"Really, they're ok. I appreciate it, though, and the tea." I smile, subconsciously running my hands over my sleeves and the bruises before reaching over to touch the glass.

"Stubborn, huh? Who'd have known?"

The playful teasing from before comes back full force with yet another of those winks. *Is he flirting with me on purpose? Why do I hope he is?*

Standing again, Joshua walks the couple of steps back to the loveseat to sit again, still not fully relaxed, although appearing less upset.

"So I have a purpose for coming by tonight. I spoke with Uncle Jonathan and Cooper about our conversation, and they both agreed that they would like to see things change, which is no small miracle, I'll have you know. They would like to meet with you tomorrow if you're available. I told them I would escort you if you could come up to give your old truck a break." Joshua's playful tone continues, accentuated by a huge grin.

"Ha! My old truck, huh? She can make it up that terrible road just as well as any other vehicle can, I'll have you know!" I shoot back, also grinning.

"I know, but we have to take care of things with such value, don't we?"

Why do I get the feeling he's talking about more than just a truck?

An unexpected blush starts creeping up my cheeks.

I shift to a more serious tone. "Well, with everything else, I haven't prepared an actual presentation, but I'm willing to wing it and thankful for the chance."

"I'm sure you'll be great. I should let you get some rest, though, so I will come back in the morning to pick you up."

My eyes close without warning. I must be more worn out than I realized.

"Thanks, Joshua. Would you like to..."

Opening my eyes, he is gone again. This unusual man slips in and out of my days like a vision without warning.

*****

Do you ever have a dream so vivid, you could swear you were awake? I am back at the farmhouse, waking up for breakfast, and I hear Mama in the kitchen getting after Cameron about his homework not being finished again. I smell eggs cooking, fresh from the hens, no doubt. Daddy walks into the kitchen with those big boots... My eyes open, and reality comes back quickly. Remembering the truth, that they're all gone, is sobering, but *why on earth do I still smell eggs*?

The clock on the nightstand is no help. I must have forgotten to rewind it last night. It's bright enough outside that it can't be early, though. I slip into my second favorite pair of jeans and a fresh shirt. Lola is kind enough to wash my laundry for me more often than I do these days, and had left these folded for me on the chair in the corner of the room. Throwing my hair up into its almost constant ponytail, I head out to the kitchen to find a small bouquet of field flowers, a fresh cup of tea, and Joshua standing in the kitchen making eggs with Matthew.

"Good morning, sleepy head." There's that wink again.

"Auntie!" Matthew jumps out of his seat and runs over to me before I even make it out of the hallway. I never get tired of this boy and his morning greetings. A hug and a kiss on the cheek are enough to lift any mood, even the solemn one my dream brought about.

"Look at the flowers! I got down the vase from the hall closet very carefully. I know you said it was Grandma's, so I didn't want to break it. Mr. Joshua brought fresh eggs and some flour, too, so we're making pancakes and eggs for breakfast. He's a really good cook. We were being extra quiet so you could sleep too, Auntie. Did we do a good job?" Matthew's excitement is bursting through as he says everything as fast as he can.

The bright yellow and pink wildflowers were a perfect match for the happy yellow paint in the kitchen. The light blue vase was one Cameron had made for our mother one year for Mother's Day out of clay in school. She gave it to Ginny on Mother's Day the year she was pregnant with Matthew, and I don't think it left that closet much since.

"You did an excellent job, Sir, now show me to those pancakes!" I say with a broad smile brought on by the infectious nature of this sweet boy's mood.

Like a true gentleman, he takes my hand to lead me the rest of the way to the tall island table in the center of the small kitchen.

Joshua is managing both cast iron pans and flips a perfectly golden pancake before turning to talk to me.

"Good morning! Lola came by to take Jamal to The Restaurant. We figured you needed all the rest you could get after all of the craziness lately. She said she'd stop back by for Matthew in a bit before we head up the mountain." Joshua takes a sip of hot tea.

I stretch my arms up and smile. "It feels like it's been years since I slept so late, I almost don't know what to do with myself. And spoiled too, this breakfast is almost too good to be true! Thank you both very much for this."

The small tabletop is already set with just one plate, napkin, silverware, and even a short glass with orange juice from the tree down the street. Joshua brings over the pan with the eggs and quickly slides them onto my plate. He has a tea towel over his right shoulder, which makes him look like a professional. *Where did he learn that?*

Two perfectly round, golden pancakes are next, and the towel comes off to lie next to the sink as he sits in the chair across from me.

"We already ate with Jamal, but you should go ahead. Enjoy it, we have plenty of time." Joshua gestures to the plate before me.

Settling in with his cup of tea, I take a moment to really see Joshua, picking up details that I hadn't seen before, maybe because of the lack of time, or the more pressing issues on my mind. Now, on this beautifully strange morning, enjoying eggs that are better than any I remember having before, I begin to notice the little things that make him different, special even. His tanned skin from time outside in the garden, or during his travels for supplies, a slightly shaggy haircut in need of renewing but in a way that almost looks like it could be on purpose, the lines by his eyes from creasing with laughter, the way his nails were kept short, not from being chewed on like some, but actually cut.

His red and black plaid shirt is clean and tucked in, even though it is well worn, much like his Wrangler jeans. He wears a pocket watch, probably his grandfather's, in one pocket, and a folding knife is clipped into the opening of the other. His lace-up boots show the work he has put them through, but are remarkably clean for someone living in the country. His shoulders are broad and strong, and ready for work. His face is handsome, but not in a flashy, chiseled, Hollywood star way, but more simple, gentle, and pleasing even with the scruff of not shaving for a day. His blue eyes are bright and kind. The type of blue that catches your breath if you're not careful. His dark brown hair is starting to show little sparkles of gray here and there, just enough to add character, and

a little mystery.

"We should probably head out soon, the elders will be waiting."

The trance is broken, and I blush, realizing he must have noticed me staring by the grin on his face. I quickly finish the last of the eggs and place my dishes in the sink.

"I'll just grab my boots."

Quickly hurrying back to my bedroom, both to escape and so we can get on the road, I grab my hiking boots this time instead of the sneakers I'd had on last time I made this trip.

Wow, that's embarrassing. How could I have gotten so swept up like that? What must he be thinking of me? Come on, Ray, pull yourself together! He's just here to pick you up and was being nice, is all. Time to be professional, you're just going to go talk to people.

By the time I walk back out into the living room, Joshua is waiting alone by the door.

"Lola just stopped for Matthew, so we are good to go."

"Ok, perfect."

I grab a canteen of water in the kitchen and the flannel near the door as we head out to the truck. It gets cooler up on the mountain sometimes, and I don't want to be caught cold. It took until we were already outside before I realized it was almost an exact match for the one Joshua is wearing. Hopefully, he didn't notice.

Looking up, I realize there is a truck at the curb.

"So, the mystery man has a vehicle after all, huh?"

Of course, that makes sense, but the tales you will come up with when you don't know the truth are amazing. He is also driving a Ford truck, although newer than mine by about 10 years. Still old enough that the EMPs didn't stop it from working.

Joshua makes it to the truck first and holds open the door for me.

"Mystery man? I don't know about that, I'm just a boy opening a door for a girl, hoping she'll get in."

He waits for me to jump in before closing the door and going around to get in on his side. The parody of a movie quote from what is generally referred to as a "chick flick" throws me off even more.

"Yes, mystery, like where did that quote come from? I mean, I never expected you to..."

"To what, enjoy a romantic comedy? I am the only child of a single mother. My range is definitely wider than the average male, especially one from the mountain."

A laugh escapes as I reply, "I can see that! Bravo! Most guys wouldn't have admitted that."

"Hmm, probably true, but then I am *the mystery man,* am I not?"

The flirtatious banter leaves me with a few butterflies in my stomach and an excited, joyful feeling at the prospect of learning more about him while we travel.

The truck starts, and the sound of the engine tells that it has been well cared for, despite its hard life on the mountain. The ride is uneventful, and Joshua makes some more light conversation about movies, trees, history, and books. He asks if I know what I am going to say to the elders, which I had better figure out pretty quickly.

Chapter Fifteen

How Important This All Is

Being with Joshua, we don't have to make the same hike up to the buildings as I did the last time I came up. Just a few minutes later, we arrive at the big building I had once seen being fired upon. A closer look shows light streaming through so many holes that there doesn't seem to be any solid wall left. Who knows how many lives have been lost here? The thought is sobering and reminds me again of how important this all is.

As we walk inside, I am surprised to see close to 100 people all jammed into a space not designed for nearly so many. It must be just about everyone from both the upper and lower folk together.

Jonathan and Cooper appear out of nowhere to greet us.

"It's good to see you again, Raylene." Cooper has on a much cleaner set of overalls and a once-white pullover shirt this time. He offers his hand to close his greeting.

"We're glad you agreed to come all the way back up here to chat with u
My nephew here has been going on about the ideas y'all talked about.
Jonathan also has a shirt today, no doubt in honor of this being a planne
get-together instead of a complete stranger coming into a private momer
unexpectedly.

"I'm honored that you would allow me to come and speak with you.
admit I thought this would be a much smaller gathering. Joshua had onl
mentioned meeting with the elders."

Jonathan chuckles. "Oh, you will just meet with us, but when peopl
found out about it, they wanted to have a look at the townie coming up her
to try to change things. Frankly, we don't get many visitors, so it's a bit of
to-do when someone does come up."

I smile, trying to quiet the nervousness filling my middle. "Well, I hope
won't disappoint. Shall we get started?"

"Straight to work, I like this girl. You better watch out, Joshua, or I'm
steal her from you."

Cooper's statement catches Joshua a bit off guard, and it's his turn t
blush. He hides it well by changing the subject to moving towards th
meeting room. I can't help but smile just a bit. "Focus, woman!" I mutter.

"What's that?" Joshua asks.

"Oh, nothing, just reminding myself of something."

Stop talking to yourself out loud!

The meeting room is really just what looks to be an old office from th
days when this building was in use. Someone had set up a few chairs, barrel
and a bench for seats. The elders consist of just nine people, mixed betwee
the two groups. Several look less than pleased to be present. *This may l
harder than I expected.*

"Alright, y'all, let's get this started. This here is Raylene. She come u
this way a while back and saw one of the unfortunate fall in the next roon
Since then, she's mentioned to Coop, Joshua, and m'self some ideas abou

how maybe we wouldn't need to do that anymore. Joshua has checked up on her and she is doin' some pretty big things down below. She seems to be the real deal. I know some o' y'all aren't too keen on an outsider comin' up here and havin' a say, but I hope you'll hear her out so we can just see what comes of it."

Stepping forward from the edge of the room, I begin, "Thank you for your kind words, Jonathan. What you've said is completely correct. There was an incident with a young man that inadvertently involved Joshua, so I came to ask for his help in saving that boy from what would have been a very serious maiming. When I walked up from the roadblock to find him, I came to the clearing just as the shots began, and when I realized the purpose, it broke my heart, as I'm sure it must yours every time that situation arises. I can't imagine how this must hurt your community and families." Several of the elders' faces reflect shame as they look away, shift in their seats, or hug their arms around themselves at this thought.

I continue, hoping to move past the sadness and bring them to the idea of potential. "During the walk through to Joshua's house, I made several observations about your land and people, and many ideas came to mind. I know that I am an outsider, and that I am inexperienced in your culture as well as the way you manage things, so please forgive my ignorance should I suggest something that is inappropriate in any way. I mean no disrespect at any point and am honored to have this opportunity.

What I'd like to do is actually walk around a bit with you and show you what I was thinking, if that would be alright."

"We'd rather stay here." A scowling, petite woman with messy gray hair in a sort of bun snaps back.

"Oh, don't be a grump, Eunice, let the girl do what she came here to do," says Coop.

"Oh alright, but we ain't going in no houses or private areas." For such a small woman, she has an effortless way of making herself seem like the boss.

When she stands, she is only maybe 5' 2" and not much more than 100 pounds. The years have taken their toll, and her once strong body is now bent forward. She wags her arthritically bent finger at me before walking out the door to go outside.

"Agreed! I'll try to be brief."

We start out walking past the building down the path that leads back towards the lower houses. There isn't much on the right side of the path, as all of the buildings seem to be on the left. Passing a couple of run-down single-wide mobile homes, we come to an open grassy area with a very old-looking field fence perimeter.

"Down through here, I see you have a few loose goats and sheep, which is excellent. I noticed that the goats all look like Kiko meat goats, though, which are not going to give you much milk after freshening. I know a farmer down in the valley who raises some excellent dairy breeds, which, when bred with your goats, will also give you babies with larger frames so they will carry more meat as well as offering more milk. I'd like your permission to broker a deal with him to see about getting you a few does that you can begin to selectively breed into the stock you already have here, which will improve the benefits as well as add to your numbers so you can harvest more from them." A couple of the older men whisper something to each other, looking like they are considering my suggestion carefully. Most of the group is hard to read, maintaining rather blank expressions.

I continue, still hopeful that something will click and interest them in a positive change. "Looking at the space you have them in, it is a decent size, but I am sure they are eating more than this piece of land can offer. There is a space a little further down that doesn't look to be cleared yet," I say gesturing further up the path toward a large area of overgrown thicket and trees. Several sets of eyes follow my hand to see what I'm referring to.

"If you were to use the animals to help clear it and use the wood harvested from some of the trees to close it in, the animals would be fed while making the work easier for you at the same time. While they're out of their current pasture, it could be planted with a cover crop, including things like clover and alfalfa, allowed to grow up a foot or so, then you can turn the animals back out into that side and plant the second pasture they were in. Eventually, you can switch them back and forth enough that the grasses would recover before being grazed again. By rotating between a couple of pastures, the land and animals will both be healthier, and you shouldn't need to supplement their feed until winter, if at all."

"Where are we supposed to get this seed? We don't have nothin' like that." One of the men in the back asks, seemingly annoyed, no doubt due to the potential impossibility of the suggestion threatening their fragile, new hope.

"My family owns one of the farms in the valley as well as the feed and farm store in town. I still have some seeds and have been working with the local farms to teach them how to save seeds from their crops so they will be able to plant each year with seed they keep from the year before. I can do the same for you."

I'm not an expert in body language, but fewer of the elders have arms crossed and scowls on their faces at this information. A couple are even nodding as if they approve and are whispering to each other. I pray this is a good sign. Catching a glance from Joshua, he smiles and throws me a quick thumbs up from under the elbow of his crossed arm. I find his presence relaxing as we continue, and I suddenly realize just how glad I am to have him there.

"I grew up with animals and farming, so I can teach a few of your people what I know, so you won't even need me to make this work. If you don't have any more questions, we can move to another spot I had some thoughts on."

We make our way back up to the building and take the path behind it, headed up towards the upper folk's side. It's hard to miss the group of people that keep peeking out from the same dilapidated houses I saw the first time I was here, and following us as we walk along.

"The creek that runs through between your two areas is perfect for surface irrigation. It'll take some work, but if you clear the large trees in the area just below the creek on the lower side, then let the sheep and goats go through the land followed by some chickens, they will both have their feed needs covered as well as help to fertilize and clean up the land there while their other pastures recover. Once they have finished, they can be moved out and the land prepared and planted. These would be shorter-term goals to help put you in a better position going forward.

Looking more to the long term, if some swales were added across the slopes, you could plant trees and fruit bushes along there to take advantage of the rainfall, and create a maze, if you will, for the animals to be grazed back and forth through."

Most of the faces appear confused, but no one is willing to ask a question and appear to look foolish.

Joshua, noticing this as well, jumps in. "If I understand it correctly, a swale is where you cut in a sort of curved trench, where the water will naturally run and be caught as it goes downhill to slow it down and allow it to soak into the soil, watering whatever is planted there, correct?"

I smile gratefully at Joshua. "That's absolutely correct! It is a great way to manage water and soil to your advantage."

"Won't them goats just eat the trees?" A previously silent elder chimes in from the side.

"That is possible without protection, yes. If you didn't want the risk of the animals damaging any of the perennial plants, you could seed these alleys with grain crops like wheat, corn, barley, and sorghum which would provide food, and wind protection, as well as strengthening the soil to avoid erosion as the water flows downhill from swale to swale."

A few elders are starting to look more interested and open to these suggestions.

"For now, you could potentially put in some quick-maturing crops in the areas that are open and closest to the stream to have something available to help fill bellies until things could be timed better next year."

"What would you plant?" asks Jonathan.

"Well, we're starting to come into fall, so things that like the cooler weather coming would be ideal. Most of your brassicas, like broccoli, cauliflower, and cabbage, would be good, as well as beets, turnips, and some of the winter-maturing carrots. I'd focus on the root crops as much as possible since they will store well for use over the winter. I have some seeds for each of those in my bag back in the truck, if you would like to have them."

Nods and murmurs pass between the elders, almost all showing signs of approval.

Coop speaks up first. "I think those seeds sound like a good deal to me." He smiles a bit my way, one of the more encouraging members of the group.

"Then they're yours," I reply, glad to have another ally.

"Again, looking forward to next year, one large pasture could be harvested for hay and other plants, so you can put up feed for the stock in the winter. Then another section would be made into a large garden area for produce using intensive gardening practices. You can use some of this for feed as well, but the majority would be put aside for your people. Then, if you plant additional fruit trees along the edge of the fields and the creek, they will basically water themselves. I have access to trees we can trim to make cutting starts for that as well."

"Where are we supposed to keep all of this grain and such?" A different man speaks up this time.

"Repairing the large building down below to be mostly waterproof would be a good option for the hay for sure. Good roofing tin is a bit harder to get my hands on now, but putting in a silo or two, or even metal grain boxes would be better for managing pests trying to get into the grain.

One way to accomplish this would be to take the wood that is cleared out of the fields and build a few log cabins. When those are done, you could move a few families from the mobile homes I saw, starting with those in the lowest repair, like the one with pallets and a tarp for the roof, then salvage the useful parts for the cabins and the tin on the outside for repairing your barn and grain storage. It would be labor-intensive, but a very useful repurposing of the materials as well as a housing improvement. I have a few men down below that are very skilled with construction, and I've been working with an engineer in a town over who I may be able to ask for some plans for something like that, if needed.

For the produce, a few root cellars can be dug near the houses on each side to store food that will keep over the winter."

"This all sounds like it will take years to get done. What about the need we have now?" Eunice is wise, even if she is grumpy.

"Excellent question. This will take as long or as short as you want it to. Some things will take years to see come to their full potential, but some can make a difference much sooner. I know that isn't a definitive answer, but the truth is, if you brought every able-bodied person out and gave them a job to do, you could have that field cleared and planted in a week or two.

Even the kids can help collect sticks and put a few boys on a rope to pull a log, and they'll move it. The only real limiting factor here is what you and your people are willing to do. I will do as much as I can, and Joshua is an excellent resource as well. In him, you have someone right here with you who can help lead you through all of this." I look at him and gesture his way, reminding the elders that he is available and able as well. Joshua sends me small smile, grateful for the mention. Several of the elders look at him as well and begin to whisper again.

"If you have a few people willing to bring a truck or two down, there are a few places in town that are abandoned but have fencing that I haven't been able to get taken down yet. The building will need to be torn down anyway, so if you collected the fencing for smaller pens for chickens, turkeys, and such, it would actually help us as well. We can collect some hoses from those houses for irrigation at the same time since they aren't being used anyway."

"Why would your people just give us good stuff, and where are all these animals supposed to come from? We don't have anything to trade for them or buy them outright. This just doesn't make sense." A woman, this time, who has been silently listening the entire time, now speaks out, sounding quite frustrated.

"The short version, they respect me. The majority of people in my area of town, as well as the farmers out in the valley, are all doing well because I've been a voice of common sense, and people listen. I've provided things to help people get started, and they have agreed to help others as part of the deal. It only does good for us to all work together, and working together has indeed done some good.

As far as where things will come from, I can provide seeds and starts for several fruit varieties from existing trees below, as well as the other crops. The animals will take a bit more doing, but you already have a start anyway.

I thought I saw a well or two below. If you need anything else to put one in, maybe closer to the animal pens, I can see what I can do to help with that, also. I'm sure hauling water is one of the things making this harder."

"So, where would we even start? Do you have plans drawn up at all?" A younger man, still very much my senior, has moved closer to the front as we've been walking, and now stops to ask.

"I don't have anything on paper, but I can work that all out with Joshua and make sure he has my thoughts on it anyway. I want you to know that I respect your positions and certainly don't want to dictate your actions. This is your land and your people."

There is a long pause while everyone reflects on what has been said. Jonathan is the first to speak.

"You've certainly given us a lot to think about. I think we'd like some time to think on these things. Give Joshua your plans and a list of what you will give us to start this work, and we'll let you know."

"That's completely reasonable, Jonathan. I will work on that right away and get it to you as soon as I can. Thank you all again for your time. I look forward to working with all of you."

The elders huddle together, obviously discussing the work ahead of them. Joshua and I begin to make our way back out of the barn.

Joshua walks next to me, pats my shoulder, and gives it a gentle squeeze. "Hey, you did great! I think they may actually do something this time. Even Eunice was starting to come around there at the end."

I smile back at him, after a deep breath, still trying to relax the nerves built up from the situation. "Thanks, and thanks for that thumbs up. I hate how nervous I become when I have to talk to a bunch of people I don't know."

Pointing out to the field, Joshua asks, "What do you say we walk around a bit and go over some more details? If it gets too late, I have a spare room you are more than welcome to use."

I nod, "We can walk around, but I should really get back tonight if that's ok. With the Sheriff and the fake soldiers around, I worry about Matty and Jamal."

"I understand, let's get this worked out then, huh?"

I can't help but notice he seems disappointed. The next hour goes quickly as we work out exact locations for the different pens, trees, and fields. He has a notebook and writes it all down so there will be something to show the elders. We even find a stand of bamboo that can be used to trellis things in a garden. It's exciting to imagine how amazing things could be here in just a short while if everyone pitches in.

Chapter Sixteen

Time for a Takeover

The next day, I meet Jamal outside of The Restaurant to walk him back to Mama Lou's after work. He is healing nicely and really doesn't need all that much help, but it makes me feel better to know that he isn't walking alone. As I head home, I can't shake the feeling that someone is watching me. I keep looking to figure out where that might be coming from with no success. Just in case, I change my route and head around the back of my house to find Steven on the other side, looking down the street as if he was the one watching me.

"Steven?"

Steven startles, jumping back, and instinctively reaching to his side where his pistol sits during working hours.

"Oh geez, Raylene! Don't you know better than to sneak up behind a body?" He relaxes considerably, no longer reaching for a weapon.

"I'm sorry, I thought I was being followed. Was that you?"

Steven closes his eyes and pinches the bridge of his nose before responding. "Look, we need to talk. The Sheriff is getting worse. He's built himself a still and is drinking even more than before. He's gone from mean to complete rage when he's drunk. He rants on and on about you and how you're going to pay for this or that. It's totally irrational and obsessive. I tried to calm him down last night, and he almost shot me for it. He can't know I'm here, I'm afraid for my family. I know we aren't really on the same side of all of this, but I thought you should know."

Before I can say anything, he leaves quickly through the back gate, running down the narrow alley behind the houses and leaving me with quite a lot of thinking to do.

*****

In the morning, I walk Jamal to The Restaurant. Joshua has brought down the rest of the books for the library, save a few, which he is using to work with any interested kids up on the mountain. Jamal and I are working on organizing them and building a cataloging system when gunshots come from right outside. Dropping low and looking out the window, I see the soldiers all armed surrounding the front entrance. I draw my pistol and notice several men have come from the back with weapons of their own.

"I know you're in there, Ray. Come out with your hands up and let's talk." The Captain demands loudly.

Lalonda appears on the other side of the shorter shelves. "Who does this guy think he is, coming to my place with guns drawn? Ray, what kind of trouble are you bringing to me now?"

Lalonda seems to be a mix of nervous and angry at this brazen person daring to issue a challenge on her turf.

I sigh heavily, frustrated with the situations inside and out, both less than ideal. "He is a man impersonating a soldier; they all are. They came to my house requesting supplies and volunteers to supposedly go fight in the outlands. I had hoped he would be reasonable when I turned him down, but it appears he has decided to go the other way instead. I'll go see what I can do."

Stepping outside, it is evident that the Captain is the only one with his heart in this mission, but the others are going to support him nonetheless.

"Captain, what can I do for you? Have you decided to take me up on my proposal?" I ask, as politely as I can muster, recognizing the danger and likelihood of escalation.

He shakes his head and scoffs. "Your proposal is a joke."

His eyes narrow, and he looks back at me before continuing.

"No, I am here to give you one last chance to give me what I want willingly, or I have decided we will just take it, starting with whatever and whoever is in there."

He motions at The Restaurant with his rifle as he begins to walk closer. I naturally back up towards the door, which sets him off even more. Before I can get far at all, he runs at me and grabs my arms, which are still sore from the last time this was done.

"Let go before one of the well-armed men in there decides you need a bullet," I say, externally appearing much calmer than I actually am.

Surprisingly, he lets go, pushing me back into the wall as he scoffs, but still looks around nervously. Lalonda has a reflective privacy tint on all of the windows, so you can't really see inside, but you can see out. This time, her paranoia may just be paying off.

"What's it going to be? Are you going to give me what I want, or am I going to take it?" The hatred in his words, practically spitting them like darts, is not lost on me. We have no more chances to try to convince this man to be rational.

"Give me a few minutes. This is not my part of town. I need to speak with the person in charge over here, but I will see what I can do. Do you need anything in particular?"

The Captain half-shouts and half-growls his next words. "We've been through that already, don't play stupid with me."

I nod and start walking toward the door. "Ok, I'll be back in a bit."

Walking back inside, I find Lalonda and her men all poised with their weapons at each of the windows.

Lalonda lowers her pistol, puts an empty hand on her hip, and then asks, "Well, what do they want then?"

"Your men, their guns, and supplies. He's set on it. I have an idea though."

Lalonda rolls her eyes and sits down in a chair at one of the tables just behind her men. "Oh, I'm sure you do. Am I going to like it?"

"I think so. What if we invite them in for a meal, but send at least half of your men to the back so they only see some of them? They know you have some, so we want them to think they know what they are facing. We can also send a few out the side door to the alley to take the vehicles if needed. It will be hard for them to retreat if they have nowhere to go. Then we pretend to discuss it all.

I had already asked the fake Captain if they would be willing to stay over here as a sort of protection for the town, but he turned me down flat. His men didn't hear the offer, though. I think we should talk about it. If need be, the rest of the men can come out and we will surround and disarm them. We can send them to jail until something can be determined to do with them. Then we move their equipment to the old police station in the center of town so that it would have the closest route to any edge of town in case it would be needed."

Lalonda is almost reclined in the chair, with her legs crossed at the knee and a single finger turning her gun around on the table as she speaks.

"I want to keep something here, after all, it is my men, my food we're talking about."

I quickly counter, we don't have much time to work this out. "What if you take a truck to add to your fleet? You still benefit, and the town keeps the protective equipment."

Lalonda leans forward into the conversation. "Ok, I'll take the truck and their weapons and ammo then."

I can't let her have all of the weapons and ammo. We would definitely lose balance in the town. "The truck and half of the weapons and ammo. The other half will go to the Hillside to help protect the town from the Northwest."

Lalonda sighs, happy enough with the deal, although trying not to show it. "Alright, deal. You go let the goons in and I'll get set in here."

I turn to the front corner, where the silent librarian has been sitting motionless the entire time. "Jamal, why don't you head home for now. We can finish this up later. Wait until they are headed in and go out the alley, ok?"

The boy nods and slowly stands to head for the side door. I wait just a moment, then open the door slowly, and raise my hands just to be sure they see me coming out as peacefully.

"I've talked to Lalonda, she runs this side of town. She has agreed to discuss it with you and your men over lunch. It's much easier to make a calm decision with food in your stomach, isn't it?"

Immediately skeptical, the Captain's eyes narrow to slits, still looking at each of the windows as if he will somehow see into one before looking back at me. "How do I know this isn't a trap?"

"Honestly, you decide how this goes. If you want peace, there will be peace; if you want confrontation, well, that's not something I have much power to stop. I do think that if everyone keeps their heads, this can go quite nicely."

"Ok, but we keep our guns." The Captain counters.

I've lowered my hands and started to make my way back towards the door. "I expect nothing less, but I'm not sure how Lalonda will feel about it."

"I don't care how she feels, it is how it is. Private, you stay here and watch the vehicles. Don't want them going for a drive without us." The Captain barks his orders at the nearest soldier.

Unused to the role of Soldier that he plays, the young man starts to protest. "But I'm…"

He's interrupted by an unexpected right hook from the Captain that sends him to the ground.

"Don't you *but* me, soldier! I said stay with the trucks, now do it!" The Captain walks off towards The Restaurant.

"Yes, *Sir.*" The young man rubs his jaw from his position now on the ground. The Captain doesn't seem to be making friends of those loyal to him any more than he is of any of us.

The front door cracks open as a signal that everyone is in place.

"Gentlemen, please follow me."

The tables have been shifted to make one large seating area in the center of the room, with several single tables around it in a circle. Lalonda's men are already seated at a few of the outer tables, which noticeably does not help the tension level, but the soldiers all take seats in the center of the room anyway. It seems most likely that their stomachs are making this decision for them. Who knows when they last had a good meal?

"I'm going to go find out what your man outside would like. No reason he can't eat as well."

Stepping outside again, I approach the supposed Private. "Hey, are you ok? That was some sucker punch!"

The Private looks down. "Yeah, I'll be alright."

"I'm really sorry he did that to you. He doesn't seem like the most reasonable guy, does he?" I ask, genuinely concerned, and also trying to find an in with this young man.

"Not really, but I think he's just frustrated." An emotion likely shared by the young man now looking off into the distance, eyes narrowed, and teeth gritting after his words.

"Oh, here is a menu. I told them I would make sure you were fed at least." I hand him a tattered old menu with most things crossed off since they can't be made anymore.

The Private reaches out to take it. "Thanks."

I lean up against the truck next to him. "So, how did you end up with this crew? You seem different from the rest."

"They recruited me on post, actually. I was visiting my uncle when everything happened. Pretty much everyone is gone, but a few of us were left. I was the only one who agreed to come, but it hasn't been much like they said it would be." The Private shrugs, a bit dejected in his new reality.

"That stinks. I've been trying to help those who were left as much as I can, but I haven't made it down to post. Honestly, I didn't think there was anyone left there. I'd be willing to help you if you want to get away from all of this. I'm sure I can find a place for you here."

The Private pauses, trying to work his way through both options, the mess he knows he's in, and the unknown of staying in this town full of strangers. "I don't know. I don't think he'll let me go."

"If I can arrange it, would you though?"

Another pause, and he begins to nod his head. "Yeah, I think I would. I don't care for the way we have had to be around people, threatening them with guns and such. I don't think this is what my uncle would have done if he were here."

I reach out and pat his shoulder. "You're probably right about that. My brother was stationed on post as well, and I know for a fact he would not have stood for this sort of thing. I think it is very brave of you to consider a different path. I'd like to make that happen for you. Your name was Jesse, right?"

"Yeah... good memory."

"Jesse, I'm going to go back inside and get you a sandwich and something to drink. Depending on how things go inside, some men may come over here. Don't fight them, ok? Just surrender if it comes to it, and you will be just fine."

"I can do that. Thank you for all of this." Jesse looks at me, sincerely grateful, with just a glimmer of hope shining through. *I hope he will be alright.*

"You're welcome, Jesse. Hang tight, and it'll be over soon."

Things don't seem to be going well inside. The Captain is obviously upset, and there are more fingers on triggers than could ever be good.

"What's going on in here?" I ask.

The Captain is all too ready to respond. "This woman you said was in charge seems to think I'm just going to hand over everything we have to her and walk out of town with nothing. You are sorely mistaken."

The Captain jumps up, aiming his pistol at Lalonda. Guns go up all over the room, each aimed at another person. If even one trigger is pulled, there would be a bloodbath.

"Whoa! Whoa! Whoa!" I raise my hands towards everyone, trying to slow things down even for a second.

"Everyone, just take a step back for a second. I'm sure there is just some misunderstanding here. We do not expect you to leave everything and walk. The original proposal that you stay and become part of our community is still on the table."

The Captain turns to look at me, almost with disbelief on his face that I could be so dumb as to not understand his simple demands.

"And I told YOU... You don't listen, do you?" The Captain half growls through gritted teeth.

"I do, and I heard you, but I did not hear your men. The offer stands for each of you to stay here where we can give you jobs, food, shelter, and you can keep your higher purpose of protecting those who can't always protect themselves."

"SHUT UP! These are MY men and you don't get to speak to them!" The Captain is now shaking his gun at me, desperation and overwhelming anger coursing through him like a drug. His hands are shaking, and his face contorted from the heaviness of everything going so very wrong. In a last attempt to accomplish his goal, he commands his men, "Let's go, boys, time to take what is ours."

"NOW!" Lalonda shouts. She and I drop as six more men spill out from the kitchen door, each armed with a semi-automatic rifle.

"WEAPONS DOWN, HANDS UP NOW! NOW! DO IT NOW!"

Lalonda's men make quick work of disarming the soldiers. The Captain glares at me with an intense hatred filling his face.

"You LIAR, you tricked me AGAIN!"

The Captain advances towards me with his hands out for my neck. Before I can even react, Bruno reaches out and pulls him backwards onto the floor by his collar and drops a knee into his chest. I'm not sure just how much Bruno weighs, but it is sufficient to hold the 6-foot-tall man securely in place. Someone pulls out zip ties, and each of the soldiers' hands is bound. Glancing outside, I can see that the trucks have all been taken, and Jesse is bound as well.

It's a couple of miles to the police station and jail, so we decide to use a truck in convoy with the Stryker and tank to haul everyone over. A few of Lalonda's men agree to help the deputies manage the new prisoners at the jail. They will all be interviewed individually to see who should be released and who is too dangerous to let go. I have a feeling only one will be left incarcerated by the time they're through.

Chapter Seventeen

Another Mess

It's been a full day since the fake soldiers were arrested, and it's time I stop by the jail to check on everyone and release Jesse. I have talked to my neighbor Brian from next door, who has agreed to take him on until a good permanent fit can be found for him. Brian is a veteran and a tough guy if he needs to be, but also grew up in the foster system and understands what it is to be alone in the world. If anyone can help Jesse make sense of this new life, it will be him.

The jail is small but has enough empty cells that we were able to separate the Captain from the rest of the men and still keep everyone reasonably comfortable. I decide to help the men interview the soldiers, and so far, two of the eight that are left have decided they really want to stay, so arrangements are already being made for them.

Of those who are still considering their options, there are only a couple who seem to be tied to the original plan of going to fight. They will need to stay here until they either come around or accept that they will need to leave peacefully, without their equipment. I desperately hope they all make a peaceful choice. There has been too much unpleasantness lately, and the idea of more violence is more than I'd like to consider at this point.

It is getting close to 5 pm again, time to get Jamal and check in with Lalonda. Entering the front doors, I see Lalonda back in her corner booth. She doesn't acknowledge me, but I go to sit with her anyway.

"Thank you for everything you did yesterday. That actually went a lot better than I expected it to," I say, hoping to have a polite conversation today.

"Well, it worked out ok for both of us, I think." Lalonda's snotty tone is mild, considering many of our interactions.

"True. I hope it will work out well for those men as well. Their leader was obviously not thinking clearly."

"That seems to be going around, it seems," Lalonda mutters.

"You mean, the Sheriff?" I ask.

"No, who..? Why would you bring him up?" She looks away and twirls her hair. Obviously, she did mean him, but somehow she seems to have fallen in love with him, maybe not the man he is now, but the man he used to be.

I remember when Brad Potter announced he was planning to run against Jim Turner, who had been our Sheriff for the past 20 years. He was only a few years older than me. We had actually been in high school at the same time, and he played football with my brother until he was injured in his senior year. He'd stayed around town and worked for his parents mostly. So many people thought he was too young to run for Sheriff, but with a football scholarship out of the question, college lost its appeal. That was 8 years ago, and he actually did a pretty good job before everything changed. No one knows how he managed to escape the invaders, but the consensus is that he was hiding, which is also why he drinks so much now. It's sad if you think about it.

"I'm sorry, I must've misunderstood you. Anyway, I just wanted to thank you and make sure we're good. I value our friendship, even if it is a little odd at times," I say this more in hope than reality, looking to a day when things may be better.

"Friendship? We are *not* friends." Lalonda says emphatically.

How lonely she seems. She's looking away again, hiding her face to keep it from telling her secrets. Maybe there is a chance for us to really become friends someday.

The bell on the front door rings, and everything changes. It's the Sheriff. He walks slowly over toward the corner booth where we are sitting. Knowing better than to stick around, Jamal quietly heads for the side door and a chance at safety.

"So I hear you ladies had quite the score yesterday. Something about tanks supposedly?" The Sheriff settles down into his normal spot next to Lalonda, his arm up over the back of the seat behind her.

I can't help but feel a little defensive, but I want to take care not to antagonize him, especially with the warnings of late.

"We just stopped people who planned to use those things against us; we didn't steal them," I reply, honestly.

"Ok, so where is everything then? I mean, shouldn't I get a piece of it if this is about the town?" The Sheriff asks, his tone shifting away from the feigned politeness he started with.

I don't see how I can reason my way through this, but I need to try.

"No one is keeping the weaponized vehicles; they are being positioned in the center of town to be used only if the town were to come under attack from someone with higher capabilities. None of us owns them," I say as professionally as I can, trying to avoid any potentially incendiary tones.

"Hmm, I see. But what about all of the weapons and ammunition? I am the law around here, it makes the most sense that I handle such things, don't you think?" A dangerous glint taking up space in his eyes - eyes that have not left me since he entered.

"I think we did a pretty decent job of it. No one was hurt, and everyone was sent to jail peacefully. We certainly would have appreciated your help, but the whole thing just kind of happened, and we didn't have time to send for you." Lalonda is unusually silent. *I almost wish she would speak, for once.*

Quickly sitting forward, arm no longer around Lalonda, the Sheriff responds bitterly. "So it's my fault that I wasn't here. Is that what you're saying? Are you *seriously* blaming me?"

"No, not at all! I am just trying to share what happened." Just a bit of my fear makes it through my voice as I find I am almost pleading in my reactions now. *I need to get out of here!*

The Sheriff begins to get louder and more animated as he speaks. This escalation can't be good at all. I start to move out of the booth and stand.

"I know what happened, you went behind my back, and now you're lying to me about what was taken so you can keep it all for yourself! You know what, I think it's time you learned some manners!"

With unexpected speed, the Sheriff is up and coming at me. This time, instead of grabbing me, he draws his pistol as if he wants to shoot me. Lalonda quickly slides in under his arm, trying to distract him as much for her pride as it could be to help me. Suddenly, he holsters his weapon and shoves her off into a nearby table, all in one motion. There are so many tables and chairs that it is impossible to get away from him quickly.

He catches up enough to grab hold of the back of my shirt. The more I resist, the more frenzied his attack becomes, and he grabs at me every way he can. He may be drunk, but his rage gives him a frightening strength.

He spins me around and slaps my face, then wraps his arms around me and wrestles me to the floor. The metallic taste of blood fills my mouth from where my cheek was sliced on my teeth just now.

His hands move over my body as though he plans to force me, and I hear fabric tearing. I keep fighting to try to push him off, even though I realize he has me pinned and I can't move his more than 200 pounds. Accepting that I can't get away down here, I close my eyes and try to calm down for just a moment to think.

My pistol fell out under the next table over, and there is no way I can reach it from here. My pocket knife... I start to try to reach for it, but can't get my arm free. Just when my hope of escape has all but gone, the Sheriff suddenly lifts off of me as if he was weightless. I open my eyes to see Bruno and Steven have pulled him back and are holding him backwards across the top of a table.

"GO!" Bruno yells.

"GET OUT!" Steven shouts.

Again, I am leaving a mess here for Lalonda and her men to clean up. Something has to change. I grab my pistol from the floor and run out towards home. Surprisingly, I don't stop until I reach my front door. It has to be the adrenaline; I haven't run that far without slowing in years. I'm glad it's dark out now, so there are fewer people to see the mess I am.

Rushing inside, I lock all of my doors, an unusual occurrence, and quickly retreat to the bathroom. The first look I get of myself is shocking, and I have to look away before I can't. I need to do something, I can't get stuck on this. I grab a big bowl of water from the kitchen and begin to wash. It seems like the smell of his drunken breath and the odor he carries from rarely bathing just won't come off, no matter how much I scrub.

Thankfully, Matty is still at Mama Lou's, no doubt thanks to Jamal telling her where I was and with whom.

The bruises on my body seem to be multiplying as the days pass, and the stress from the week is catching up with me. With no more that I can do about it tonight, I head to bed and cry while I pray myself to sleep.

Chapter Eighteen

The Coming

The Sabbath has come back around, and I am determined to take time out to spend with my Bible today. I don't always get the chance to so much as look at it, most days. Pastor still preaches on Saturdays, and I decided to go to the sermon at the last minute.

Amazingly, I still have a dress hiding in the back of my closet. It's a cream-colored, knee-length number with a small, elegant, pink flower pattern across it. This and my favorite pair of cowboy boots will have to do. I can't remember the last time I wore a dress, the time since The Coming feels as though it is all the life I have ever known.

The main service starts in 20 minutes, I'll have to move if I don't want to be late. I pin half of my hair back with the only two bobby pins I can find, and thankfully catch a look at myself in the mirror before I head out the door. Seeing the bruises all over my arms, I run back into my room for the pink, fringed wrap Grandmama crocheted for me for my 16th birthday. It'll have to do. Looking at it reminds me of family and home. I sit on the edge of the bed, running my fingers over the textures of the wrap, lost in thought for a moment. If only my sweet mama could see me now. She was always so proper and careful with her look, even at home on the farm.

One day, one of the milk cows startled as Mama was milking her, sending Mama and the milk both flying. She was fine, but nothing in that barn breathed a sound as she stood up, handed Daddy the bucket, and went to wash up. I thought Daddy was going to bust trying not to laugh, and all I could think was how glad I was that I wasn't the one who made her wet and dirty.

It took a while for her to laugh over it, but once she did, it became a classic story around the table. Oh, how I miss her brushing my hair and braiding it on Friday nights so it would be curly for fellowship the next day. It was already pretty curly on its own, but in a wild way that used to fluster her every time she saw it. I glance up at the mirror over the dress. Not much has changed.

*****

Walking into the service, I am surprised to find that just about every seat is taken. I don't remember it ever being this full before, but I'm glad so many are coming to hear the teaching. Today, Pastor is speaking on John 14, and I am reminded that no matter how crazy life gets, I can still be peaceful. The message washes over me, cleansing in a way the washing I attempted yesterday never could. I feel free and calm. I need to make time to come more often.

Leaving the service, I walked home with Mama Lou and Lola, who had brought Matthew since he had stayed the night with them. I take the time to catch them up on some of the things that have happened. Everyone talks to Mama Lou, so she helps spread the word to neighbors when things need to be said. The Sheriff will have a much harder time getting into the neighborhood as soon as Mama Lou starts talking, and if he does come, people will know it isn't a friendly visit. Her friendship and guidance are a large part of why the hillside stands with me and why our section of town is arguably the most prosperous.

Mama Lou is somewhere in her forties, but don't let her know I said that. She is a proud, God-fearing black woman who originally came from the Deep South. I've never met anyone quite like her. She has a heart for everyone she meets, and I can't imagine how anything would work without her. She has become my mentor and often my confidant.

Going back into my room to change into something more comfortable brings me back to the reflective mood I experienced this morning. Looking back on the past, it's strange to trace just how things came to be the way they are. I never sought a leadership position in the community; it just happened. I was in town when the invaders came, running the store so Mama and Daddy could be free to run the farm just outside of town. The town was overrun before anyone really knew what was happening.

Suddenly, everything electric went out, and fires started burning around town. Within minutes, you could hear the hum of advanced vehicles that carried beings in armor reminiscent of a sci-fi movie. To this day, no one knows where they actually came from or why they came. They crippled us, then moved on until everything anyone heard was that the world was set back a couple hundred years, only with people that have a lot less skills.

None of us could discern that they wanted anything. They only killed those who fought back, almost as a self-defense response. It seemed like no one was taken or hurt if they were passive. They set certain boundaries, and as long as you stay on the right side, you are safe and free to live as you choose. It's been months since the last time I saw one. They had come back into town in a show of force after a failed attack in the outlands led by a group of men from around our town. As long as we follow their rules, they basically leave us alone, which is somewhat nice anyway.

My brother Cameron was stationed at the Army post just outside of town when they hit. We heard that the soldiers who tried to fight back were quickly wiped out. The invaders' weaponry was highly advanced and seemed to disintegrate anything it hit, including people, leaving those left behind without a body to find or bury.

Cameron's wife, Ginny, had passed away during childbirth, and his son was with me at the store that day. We went to his house afterwards, hoping he would find us there, but he never did. I left Matthew with Mama Lou and took a bike to ride the 15 miles out to the farm. Mama and daddy were gone as well; I'm guessing they put up a fight, too. It's a hard thing to realize you are all but alone in the world like that. All of my close family, except this precious little boy, was just... gone.

There weren't many animals left anymore; my parents had been closing down a lot of the farm operations, hoping to start traveling some in the next year or so. Mama hadn't been well in a long time, and they had saved up for most of their lives to go see Europe. Daddy figured he'd better get on it, or it wouldn't happen. Sadly, this worked out as I would not have had any way to manage enough feed for a farm full of animals by myself, especially without the aid of electricity and equipment.

I let the cow and a couple of goats out to the pasture, unable to start the tractor, I would have needed to get them a 1-ton bale of hay to eat. There was a small stream out there they could drink from, and the grass was tall at least. The chickens were already loose in the yard, and the cats were used to fending for themselves.

I gathered a few of my things, some of the weapons and ammo, some clothes from my room, and the food that was worth taking. I threw the scraps that would waste in the fridge out to the chickens. At least someone would eat it. The remaining weapons went out to the barn, thinking maybe if they are hidden well enough, they won't be found, and they could be a second stash just in case.

I hadn't even thought about the old truck, but when I saw it, I decided to check it, and it started. Having a vehicle changed things. I loaded up all of the remaining grain and caged the chickens to take with me, along with nails, a couple of rolls of chicken wire, and a few boards. It wouldn't be hard to put together a simple coop, and the eggs could prove helpful if I could get them to lay. If not, they could go in a pot.

Finally loaded, I drove it up the hill beyond the house to what was once my grandparents' house. Grandma had built an amazing medicinal herb garden that would undoubtedly come in handy. Gathering all of the pots, I took sections of each plant and plenty of soil to keep them happy for a while. They went into the bed far enough from the chickens that they should still be in one piece once all back to town to stay at my brother's house for now. I had a feeling it would be better to be in town for a while.

On the way back, I decided to stop off at the Joneses' place and found them home. I told them I let the few animals left out, and they were welcome to them. I didn't know that I would be able to come back and forth very often. Mr. Jones and my daddy grew up together and were great friends all their lives. I hated to see his face when I told them they were among those who had disappeared. I needed the hug that came next about as much as he did. It was all I could do not to break down and bawl right there under his massive arms. I told them I had Matthew and I needed to get back. I was glad they were ok.

Making it back into town was easy enough, and getting everything into the house was fine. Matthew was used to spending time with me and settled right down as I came in and relieved Lola. I hoped to start on building the coop first thing in the morning, but when I woke up, I found that someone had come during the night and stolen the chickens right out of the yard as well as all of their supplies.

It's hard to pray for others when you have seen so much loss in such short time, but as angry, hurt, and sad as this event made me, I did pray for them. I prayed for grace and conviction for the wrong, and ashamed as I am to admit it, I threw in a bit about God returning His vengeance on wrongdoers. Looking back, it is probably better in some ways. I don't have much time to care for them anyway.

During the weeks that followed, a few more people tried to scout into the outlands without weapons to figure out why there is a boundary there. They also never returned. So we live our lives as best as we can where we are. The world itself almost seems to hold its breath waiting for something else to happen, but so far, it's just surviving the aftermath in this crazy age, the same as us. The farms outside of town have done what they can to provide food, but without power to pump water for mass irrigation, that isn't nearly as much as it used to be. Even with food to sell, people don't have much to buy with.

Society has had to return to a bartering system. One of the early dilemmas I was able to help work out was trading the goods in my family store for sustainability items like different seeds, tools, really anything useful I could, then finding ways to employ them on the Hillside. People can use the tools to make repairs, and in trade, I ask for favors like odd repairs or projects to help some of the orphaned kids.

The seeds went to start small gardens that are easier to water since it is less to manage. I taught each of them how to save seeds from the produce. They, in turn, must share those seeds and the knowledge with their neighbors. We were able to put in a few hand pump wells around town to help draw up water in more locations, so it isn't so hard to transport to homes. Overall, people listened to reason, even if it took a while. We all need someone to lead sometimes, to make some sense out of the chaos. This time it just happened to be me.

Chapter Nineteen

Windy Days

It has been almost two weeks, and the work is completed on the first set of windmills in Carlsburg. As agreed, we are going to pick up two of them, one for us and one for Harrison. Given the situation with the Sheriff, we take a few extra men and plenty of firepower, although I pray it doesn't come to that.

Some of the handier men in the community have been working on preparing a site for the windmill near the center of town, close to the old power station. It lands in a lot technically within the Hillside portion of town, which is still a sore spot with Lalonda, but given the power grid setup, it was the logical choice. The lot used to be a sports field in the city park with plenty of open space to add more windmills as they can be made, which will go a long way to powering the town again.

In a surprising stroke of generosity, Lalonda has been feeding the men working on setting up the system each a meal every day they are working, and the hillside has been supplying them with goods to go home with in the evenings. The Sheriff is naturally doing nothing, but a promise is a promise, so his section is being done as well.

Heading out to Carlsburg goes well enough. Andy comes out of the shop with a star-quality smile to greet us. Their windmill is up and already working to run the manufacturing plant. With power again, many of the machines will have the ability to begin to create new parts for things. This deal has helped to bring life back to their town, and they are ever grateful.

"It's good to see you, Ray!"

"You too, Andy. Looks like you're in a good mood." Smiling so big back feels odd after so many hard days lately, but it is impossible to be around so many lifted spirits without catching a bit of the happiness myself.

Andy nods enthusiastically as he leads me back into the workshop to his desk, where we met last time. "I am! This deal is working out very well, and we are already seeing a difference in what we can do. The increased morale around town is a breath of fresh air many of us desperately needed."

"I can tell. It's almost floating in the air around here. I'm hoping for a similar response when we get ours going as well."

"This thing won't give everyone back their AC and internet, so I hope they realize that. The one we have is mostly going towards the plant, so more things can be made and trades pursued. Really, it isn't even enough to manage the draw for the larger machines, but it is a good start."

Reaching into a stack of papers on the desk, Andy sorts through until he finds what he is looking for.

"I've made up a list of what we should need to make another set of three, which should be a decent standing list for as many as they will have parts to supply."

Taking the paper from him, I glance it over quickly before looking back up at Andy.

"Understood. I will be sure to let the guys in Harrison know to keep putting sets together, which we can pick up at each delivery."

"I appreciate that." Andy is still looking through the papers and stops at another before offering it to me as well.

"I also have a secondary list of a few things we could really use for a couple of our own projects that they may have as well."

My smile turns down just a bit. This is unexpected, and after the way the two groups argued at The Restaurant, I'm not so sure Marshall will appreciate having this dropped on him.

"I can take it to them, but they are going to want something for it. Do you have anything in mind? I can't waste fuel driving back and forth negotiating, especially if I can just make the one scheduled trip."

Andy nods and gestures behind me. "I figured we would need to give them something. I have a couple of the guys pulling out a present for them right now."

Looking back outside of the building, a large trailer is being brought out, pulled by two men. Andy and I walk out to have a closer look.

It appears to be a metal wagon of sorts, only on a much larger scale. It has a winch in the front, a hydraulic lifting arm salvaged from a cherry picker, and hydraulics to raise the front like a dump bed. Where the men who pulled it around stand, it appears two horses could be hitched as well, but the center bar between them also has a 2" coupler for a pretty standard ball hitch.

I stick my fingers on each hand into my pockets and try to replace my smile. "That is a wonderful trailer, I'm sure they will find it very useful."

Andy runs his hand along the side, proudly. "If they agree to the parts list as it stands, then you may leave the trailer in good faith. If not, then we ask that you consider finding an alternative source for the parts, and you may keep it in trade. If this is unsuitable, then please return it to us and we will find another way. I know it is extra weight to pull, but I expected you would rather try it in one trip than go back and forth."

I raise my brows and nod in agreement. "Ha! You know me better than I thought. Thank you for all of your hard work. I will do what I can to get you the parts listed here, but it will probably take us a couple of days, as they will need time to get them together also."

Andy smiles again, still in the good mood he was in when we arrived. "Not a problem, we will work on preparing for the next load in the meantime."

The windmills are loaded, and the wagon is hitched to one of the trucks. I have the lists from Andy, and the engineer we brought with us has been brought up to speed on the installation and function of the windmills, so Andy won't have to send his guys with us after all. I wave as we leave and am thankful that this part of the day has been a success. Hopefully, things continue to go smoothly.

Pulling back into town, we draw quite a crowd. People have been whispering about this project for weeks and, in some ways, may not have expected success. Things seem to be going well until the Sheriff shows up at the park in his now normal drunken state. I wish I was surprised, but after our last run-in, I've learned that he has a knack for destructive and dangerous behaviors and the worst timing for carrying them out. He shouts obscenities not worth repeating and pulls his pistol, waving it in the air and pointing it at random people.

A shot is fired at the trucks, possibly on purpose, but likely an accident as he trips over an unseen hole in the ground. The crowd quickly runs to get away from him, and before he can get back up, one of Lalonda's men hits him on the head with the grip of another pistol, leaving him unconscious. Now that the imminent danger of being shot has gone, I go over to check his head for a wound, which thankfully is just a bump and not bleeding at all.

Looking up at the deputy next to me, I offer instructions, "Steven, you should get him home and leave someone with him to make sure he comes around alright. If you can get a bit of ice from Lalonda's, it will help with the bump he has started, and if possible, please try to get him to sober up some."

He doesn't look too sure about what I've said, but the honor he has tried to hold onto through so much adversity will press him into doing the right thing anyway. He reaches down with another deputy, and they begin to haul the Sheriff off to a cruiser.

"We'll try," Steven says as they shuffle away.

With the Sheriff gone, work resumes to finish unloading the windmill. We leave a few armed men with the installation team just in case anything else should happen.

As long as this day has already been with the pickup and the uncomfortably eventful installation of our windmill, the third still needs to be delivered to Harrison. Pulling into the edge of town, Marshall and his brother Jack meet us to head to the installation site. They have a place to set up the windmill in an empty lot near the edge of town, and the prep work looks like it has been done well.

Jumping down from the large truck, I smile and address Marshall first.

"It's good to see you again, Marshall. Are your people as antsy to get this thing going as ours have been?"

Marshall smiles back, also excited at the prospect of returning a piece of normal to the world.

"Probably. I've had at least one person asking after it every day since your trucks pulled out of the scrap yard a couple of weeks ago. I'll just be glad to see what it can do."

"I saw the one in Carlsburg set up. It's already helping to run part of the plant there. Andy mentioned that they would be ready for another load of

parts as soon as they can be gathered. He gave me a list that he mentione
can be a standing list for as long as there are parts to put towards it."

Marshall's smile turns to a somewhat skeptical daring.

"Let's see how this first one does before we dive in all the way, I think."

"Understandable! I had our engineer fuss with setting ours up before w
headed over to make sure he had a good handle on it to teach your men a
well, and it seemed to be creating a charge in some of the batteries we ha
gathered. It was pretty exciting to watch."

Marshall looks surprised. "That fast, huh? Well, maybe we will get
glimpse of that here, too."

"Maybe!" I smile back, hoping Marshall will be in a good enough moo
for the next part of the conversation.

"Andy had also mentioned that he had a couple of other projects in th
works that they would like to trade for parts to complete if y'all would b
willing. He sent along a really ingenuitive trailer that can be pulled by mer
horses, or hitched to a vehicle as a trade for it. I think it would help a lc
with moving parts and such, but could also be good for harvesting project
if you have any larger fields or orchards to handle."

"Seems like Andy may have some expectations of us that aren't quit
fair," says Marshall's foreman, Jack, who has his arms crossed and a dee
scowl covering his face.

"We aren't interested in being taken for everything we have, then left i
the dust," Marshall grumbles.

I thought this might happen. "I see your concerns. They aren
completely unexpected. Would you like to see the list to help decide if it is
fair trade? I can show you all of the trailer's capabilities first if you'd like
better idea of what you will be getting."

Marshall shakes his head and kicks the dust around his feet.

"I don't know. I guess it just seems fishy that he has this whole thing all set and we didn't even know about it." Marshall's scowl and stubborn streak were both firmly set in place.

"I don't have any benefit in this, Marshall. It's just goodwill towards neighbors, but I am willing to help you guys out with the hauling of everything. I think the thought here was to be as efficient as possible, considering how hard it is to communicate without traveling and expense. If the trailer isn't something you are willing to accept, is there something else you would find worth a trade?"

Marshall runs his hand through his hair, stressed by this change in plans. "Honestly, I don't know, maybe I just need time to think it over."

I reach into my back pocket for the papers Andy gave me. "Fair enough. Let me give you the lists, and we'll come back in a couple of days for the parts for the next set of windmills, if nothing else. I'd like to leave the trailer as well, so you can try it out and see if it will be a good fit around here. Sound okay?"

Marshall's features have softened, but he still looks noticeably irritated.

"Yeah, we'll have the windmill parts ready. No guarantees with that trailer though, I still don't like how this is going down."

I nod in agreement and offer my hand to shake his. "Thank you. I understand and I appreciate your efforts in working with us. See you soon."

It would be so much simpler if everyone saw the value in continuing to trade and work together. At least he let me leave the trailer. I'm sure taking it back to town would just cause more problems with Lalonda and the Sheriff, how I wish for easier days.

Chapter Twenty

School's In Session

Coming back from dropping Matty off at Mama Lou's, I find the Embry twins unexpectedly stopping for a visit with The Boss, Justin, and his cousin Cole. *What are they all doing at my house?* I decide to brush off the confusion of this unusual encounter and choose a pleasant tone instead.

"Hey guys! Did we have a meeting today? I apologize if that is the case; things have been a bit crazy."

I stop to open the front door to the house.

"Please come in."

The group files into the living room, much too small for so many at once. "No meeting, we would like to talk about the school idea if you have some time, though." Boss is the one to speak, as before.

"Sure, Justin, y'all sit down where you can. Can I get you some water?" I head to the kitchen before they can answer.

"Yes, ma'am."

Reaching the kitchen sink, I collect five glasses of water and walk the short distance back to the living room, handing one to each of the kids before taking my favorite seat.

"You said you wanted to talk, does that mean you've come to a decision?" I ask, looking toward Justin for an answer.

"A few of us have talked it over and think your idea could be worth trying out. There are a lot of kids, with more joining here and there, and it's a lot of mouths to feed." Justin is sitting on the loveseat next to Cole and leaning forward with his elbows on his knees.

"I imagine so. Would you guys like to take a trip over to the school so we can maybe work out exactly where what should be done to get it started? Depending on your numbers and how many are able to help, we may be able to get you guys moved in within a week or two."

Justin nods, "That sounds good, let's do it."

We take my truck to the school even though it is only about two miles from the house. With things being the way they have been, spending the extra gas is well worth having access to a vehicle. Pulling up to the front, it's easy to see that some work has already started and that there is still a lot to be done.

I turn to Justin, who is in the front seat with me. "So, I have a confession. I was really hoping that you would say yes, so I asked some of the people in the community, whom I had already been talking to about working with you guys, to come by and see about starting on getting this place going. Obviously, there is still work to be done, but I hope this shows you that we are serious about this."

Justin turns around to take in the whole view as we walk towards the main entrance of the high school. The glass making up one of the front doors has been broken out, and graffiti has been drawn on the remaining glass, as well as the walls, no doubt by some of the kids who may now come to live here.

Opening one of the functioning doors, we walk into the front lobby where broken glass from the door and trophy cases has been swept up into piles. Many of the trophies are damaged or missing, and there is more graffiti on the walls here as well.

Justin is the first to speak. "You aren't kidding about this place needing work. Who is going to supervise things here? I don't care much for taking orders from adults anymore." His skeptical tone is clear, but still respectful.

"I don't think you should take orders, but perhaps instruction and direction would be acceptable. I recognize fully that you have taken on a very adult role, and I respect that. The adults who will be a part of this will likely give each of you directions as you learn from them and work together. It would not be meant as orders but more organization. Does that sound like something we can do?"

Peeking down hallways, Justin asks, "As long as it stays respectful as equals, that's fine. Is there someone here now who would be organizing the work? I'd like to see who we're dealing with."

"We can definitely check around. People have been coming on their own time for now, until the need for a schedule might come up. Let's wander and see if we can find anyone. We can also work out some lists of things to be done while we go."

I find some loose paper and a clipboard from the front office, and after checking a few of the pens, I find a couple that work.

"Why don't I give you some of this paper? Part of organizing will be working out how many beds we need for males and females, as well as family groups, so we can figure out what needs to be collected as well as work out how the rooms will be assigned."

"I'll work on that later and get it back to someone here." Justin hands the clipboard to Cole.

"Fair enough."

Walking down the main hall, we make a left turn into the freshman hall. It is obvious someone tried to break into several of the lockers. Strewn papers, books, and trash have been swept up into another pile to be picked up later. Thankfully, there are skylights and windows giving plenty of light without needing electricity.

I turn to the group as we begin to explore the hall and express my main goals for the tour. "I have some thoughts as we go through the school, but they aren't necessarily in order of importance, just geography. Obviously, the priorities will be in the more immediate needs like shelter and food, but I wanted to propose some longer-term goals so we work on going in the right direction with the spaces we have here, if that makes sense."

The first room we come to is a large classroom once used for history class. Its large, open space gives it the capacity to be used for just about anything. The chairs are all combination desk and chair setups, so they will be best used in a classroom setting. We briefly look in and then keep walking, stopping at each doorway to glance at the contents and condition.

"I know you older boys are as familiar with these halls as I am, so you know what is basically in each of these rooms. My initial thought is that this hall can be for classes, and the classrooms can be worked out later. I am hoping to be able to have basic classes for the younger children to learn simple things like reading, writing, math, etc., the types of basic things they need to understand. Then we'd add the vocational classes somewhere in here for animal husbandry, carpentry and construction, electricity and wiring, and a room for the much younger kids that can be set up as a type of preschool.

There are a couple of teachers who had worked at the elementary school before who have said they would be happy to work with the younger kids. They have already gone to their old classrooms to collect supplies since we will probably not use the elementary school at this point. We can move on to the sophomore hall, where I was thinking we can begin to designate dorm rooms."

"Yes, please. Where the classes go doesn't matter much to me, so if you guys want to work all of that out, that's fine." Justin adds.

"Ok, let's move on then."

Heading to the sophomore hall reveals more of the same mess. The group is quiet going forward, with the only answers coming from Justin.

"Ok, so this hall should have ten rooms as well as the sophomore lockers. There is also access to the freshman and sophomore boys' locker rooms, where showers may be possible with some tinkering, so it makes sense to house the boys in here. I think it would be pretty easy to fit up to six sets of bunk beds around the edges of each room, leaving the center open. The lockers can be emptied and reassigned so each person has a place to put their personal items. There are also lockers in the locker room that can be used for hygiene items."

"What about the really young boys? We have a couple as little as three."

I try to hide my surprise. These boys have been handling so much.

"If they have siblings, I propose the sibling groups have rooms in the junior hall where they can stay together if they choose to. They can utilize the girls' locker rooms along that hall for showers. The girls not in a sibling group can then have the senior hallway and the locker rooms there."

Justin laughs, "I'm sure they'll love using the senior boys' showers and lockers. I'm not sure it is possible to air that room out enough to stop it from smelling like teenage boy funk."

The first jovial comment catches me a bit off guard, and I can't help but chuckle a bit. *Hopefully, this is a sign he is beginning to trust me.*

"Well, Isabelle, what are your thoughts?"

Suddenly putting her on the spot reveals big eyes and a somewhat startled look as if she is afraid to have an opinion. Her eyes begin to dart between Justin and me, trying to figure out what she should do.

"Whatever you guys think is fine with me."

"Sweetie, you can say what you think; no one will be mad." I reach out to pat her shoulder, hoping to reassure her.

Isabelle stutters, "I... well... I would like to use a girl's shower, but I'd be happy to use whatever we can."

Her nervous glances continue. *Maybe I shouldn't have asked her.*

"See, I told you!" Justin laughs again.

Justin's knack for problem solving and detail is impressive, and lends to the reasoning behind his leadership role for the group.

"Yes, you did. We will have to find a way to make do. The only other option I can think of would require people wandering all over the building to get to specific showers, which isn't very efficient. Perhaps this requires more thought as well. Let's check out the cafeteria."

We walk back towards the office and take another left turn, which leads to yet another hallway taking us to the cafeteria and gym located in the center of the large square that is the high school. The two rooms come up on either side of the hallway and meet in the center with a heavy set of double doors in each direction.

Entering the cafeteria, it is obvious that a meal was in progress when the invaders came. Trays, dishes, and long-ruined food are all over the tables and floor, still waiting for their turn to be cleaned up.

"So this room will need to be a priority for sure. One of the classes will actually be taught here by a woman who used to cook for a restaurant and is used to making large amounts of food. She will teach culinary arts and manage the meals here for older kids who will eventually take it over from her. She is also working with the agriculture teacher, who is going to head up the gardens and any animals you guys end up with, to plan out what will be needed to feed everyone. The list of how many kids and approximate ages will help with that planning."

"I can do that. I'll send it either to you or back here with these two." Justin gestures towards Isabelle and Franklin.

"That's perfect. Do you have any questions or other thoughts we should discuss now?" I ask.

Justin takes another look around the cafeteria before we start walking back to the front. "When do you want us here to start working on things?"

"As soon as you are able. The cleaning work is pretty obvious, so even if no one is here, there is plenty that can be done. It would be good to start working on collecting beds and such once we have numbers. We will probably just start with houses near the school that are abandoned, then work out from there. If anyone wants their own bed, we can definitely try to make that happen as we go. I'd say that can happen in maybe another week or two, depending on how the cleanup and such goes."

As we reach the front doors, Justin nods, seemingly pleased with the way things are going. "Let's plan two weeks, so I can get the information together."

"That sounds great. Thank you for going through with me. I am really excited to see this project work out." We part ways, the children going their way as I turn back to go mine.

Chapter Twenty-One

The Sheriff is Coming Home

Jamal has been healing well over the past couple of weeks. He isn't quite back to his old self, and I still walk with him to and from the restaurant as often as I can. Lalonda and her men seem to mostly ignore him anymore, so he is probably safe from another beating from them at least. We are no longer using the poultice, but we do wrap him in some clean fabric to help support his broken ribs as they finish healing. He has been sleeping back at Mama Lou's, but with all of the supplies with me, we stop to wrap at my house each afternoon.

"The Sheriff was real loud about you today, Miss Ray. He made Miss Lalonda all kinds of mad with the way 'e been going on 'bout you. I'm startin' to worry 'e's gonna do somethin' 'bout it one a these days." Jamal's genuine concern is evident in his tone.

I can't help but frown. "Thank you for the warning, I hope dearly that you are wrong. Things are hard enough without us all going after each other."

"He needs to go away, though. Things at the library were slow before but with him always hangin' 'round, almost nobody be comin' in for anything. Miss Lalonda don' see it, but he be hurtin' ever'body." Jamal winces and gasps slightly as the wrap goes around his chest.

I finish wrapping his chest again and help him up from the bed.

"I have some things for Mama Lou, if you don't mind taking them with you. They aren't heavy."

Walking into the kitchen, I hand him a small cloth bag with some fresh tomatoes, green beans, and squash I picked earlier in the garden.

I open the door to let Jamal out to head home, just as Steven was about to knock. He rushes inside, out of breath, and quickly closes the door behind him.

"He's coming here. Now!" He says, pacing hurriedly.

"Who is? The Sheriff?" I ask, shocked and a little frightened.

"Yes! He's all fired up, convinced that you are the one who hit him on the head at the windmill installation, even though you were on the other side of the field. I tried to talk him out of it, but he's lost it!" Now, at the window, peeking out of the crack in the curtains, and biting his nails.

"Do you know how much time we have?" I ask as I look out the window next to him.

"Not much at all, I ran, but he has the cruiser." He looks at me with the same scared look I am feeling.

I look at Jamal. "Go home, Jamal, tell anyone you see on the way to get home, too. This may be a bigger fight than I'd like."

Turning back to Steven, "Thank you for the warning, Steven. You should go out the back so he doesn't see you, just in case." As I escort him to the kitchen door, I pull him back to face me.

"I will not forget the risk you have taken to help us."

Just as the door closes, I turn to grab Daddy's favorite shotgun from the top of the baker's rack and check to be sure it is loaded. The siren of a police car gets louder as it roars into the neighborhood and stops right in front of my house.

I don't want this fight, but given the way things have been escalating, it was likely to happen somewhere eventually. Facing a madman anywhere isn't pleasant, and as much as I don't want him in the house, meeting him on the street is not exactly tempting either. Saying a quick prayer, I move towards the door when it slams open, revealing the face of a completely unstable man. The scent of alcohol and body odor takes over the room with as much force as the door slamming into the wall. Raising the shotgun to my shoulder, just as I was taught, I want to command him to leave, but that same ugly sneer crosses his face, and he starts in before I can get any words out.

"You're not going to shoot me, you don't have it in you. You forget I've known you pretty much your entire life, Ray, and you are too much of a *sweetie* to ever hurt someone else."

His words are dripping with sarcasm and a hatred I can't imagine the origin of.

"Besides, I'm the Sheriff now, not just some boy hanging out at a game with your brother, and this means you can't shoot me." Tapping his badge, still amazingly on his chest, to emphasize his point.

"Brad, I never realized you had such feelings for me before. I always expected that you were interested in the older girls at school, like Melody Turner," I say honestly, and as calmly as I can with this surge of adrenaline coursing through me.

He takes a couple more steps into the house as he looks around the room, smearing a dirty hand across his face like a schoolboy who refuses to use a tissue.

He sees the wildflowers I had found on my doorstep a couple of days earlier, presumably from Joshua, and before I can even consider his intentions, he backhands the vase, sending it crashing to the floor. He turns, obviously enraged, and begins shouting.

"You're seeing another man behind my back! You always were a tease for as long as I've known you! Well, there will be no more teasing ever again." I try to speak in calming tones. I want to explain that they were just from a friend when he begins to rush at me.

"I never meant to... Stay back! Stop!"

Before I can even think, the fear-filled memory of the last time he rushed at me takes over, and I squeeze the trigger. He is knocked back onto the floor, gasping for air from the damage done to his torso. Dropping the gun, I run to his side to try to stop the profuse bleeding. I'm so focused on the wound, I don't see the pistol in his hand next to me, rising up towards my head. Someone runs in and grabs the gun from his hand right before he can shoot me.

"No-no-no, Stay with me! This wasn't supposed to happen! Why did you have to do this? Why?" For all of my pleading, the truth is that it was a good shot, and he was gone within just a couple of breaths.

I feel myself being pulled away and standing up, but everything is a blur. My mind knows that I am in shock, but I feel as if I am trapped inside of myself, powerless to stop it or pull myself back into reality. All I can see is the blood all over my hands, the looped replay of the last few moments, and the man dying on the rug in the middle of the living room floor. Next thing I know, I'm at the kitchen sink and someone is helping me to wash my hands. Why is time moving so strangely? Everything is disorienting, and I still don't see who is helping me. I keep washing, but the blood doesn't seem to come off. What has come off just seems to be spreading to everything around it like a contagious disease. *Why won't it come off? Why can't I feel clean?*

More people have come in now, probably neighbors, Jamal warned, or maybe people who heard the shot and saw the Sheriff's car out front, but I don't see them either. Looking down, I see blood all over my shirt and jeans. I need to get them off now. This can't be real. I need to get all of the blood off, and then things will be okay again. My frenzied hands are clumsy and shaking as I try to unbutton my pants and undo the snaps along my outer shirt.

Seeing my panic, the mystery person pulls me into my bedroom and begins to help. Had I had my wits about me, I would have been mortified at the idea of someone seeing me like this, but I was far from able to manage that much of a thought. Once my stained clothes were off, they helped me into bed and disappeared. A few minutes later, a cup of lavender, chamomile, and valerian root tea arrives, and someone doses me with a few drops from my bottle of Rescue Remedy from the far room I use as an infirmary. I faintly hear a voice telling me to rest, but it sounds so far away.

The next morning, I woke up feeling groggy and somewhat confused. Was it all a terrible dream? Going into the bathroom, I find my outfit from yesterday hung over the shower curtain to dry. Someone had washed out the blood stains. It was not a dream. I had killed Brad Potter, the Sheriff, the boy from school, my brother's friend, someone's son. This would only mean bad things, possible retaliation from the south side of town, problems with Lalonda... would anyone accuse me of murder and send me to jail, or worse, the outlands? I need to get dressed. I need to figure this out... I need.. I need help.

I rush back into my room to dress and hear a light knock on the door. Surprised that someone would be in the house, I crack open the door to find Joshua.

"Are you ok? Can I get you something to eat?"

I don't remember him being here, but then everything is still jumbled and out of sorts. Everything except the terrible moments yesterday, when my life changed forever.

I am still struggling with reality, and I back away from the door. Seeing my confusion, he gently helps me to the edge of the unmade bed to sit.

"I came in yesterday. Do you remember what happened yesterday?" He asks, with an obviously worried look.

"You mean, the Sheriff?" I manage to whisper into my lap. It's so hard to breathe every time I remember...

"Yes, he was coming at me... I didn't mean to shoot him; it just happened. I tried to stop the blood... So much blood..." My eyes are open wide and won't blink, I swallow hard, trying to clear the lump in my throat enough to whisper again.

"All I can see is his body and the blood on my hands." Heavy tears fall as he quickly moves to kneel in front of me and covers my hands with his.

"No one blames you, Ray. He was crazy! He would have killed you! Even in his dying moments, he was still trying to shoot you. I came in just in time to stop him. Any good he ever had in him was long since replaced by evil. There wasn't anything to be done. Look at me... please?"

He touches my chin and draws my eyes away from my hands to his face. "This was not your fault!"

Finally, the torrent of pent-up tears begin to fall. Before I know it, I have sunk to the floor with Joshua, sobbing into his chest so hard it hurts. Sobbing for the life I have taken, for the innocence lost, for the heartache of so many months of holding it together through problems and crises, being strong for everyone around me. Too much tragedy, too much loss, too much sorrow. It's all been sitting there under the surface, waiting for its turn to hold my attention. He picks me up onto the bed and sits with me, still holding me with such gentle, understanding arms. I finally feel safe here.

Chapter Twenty-Two

A Trial in the Park

With the Sheriff gone, Steven is next in line to run the South side of town. The threat of a miniature civil war looms heavily as those irrationally loyal to the Sheriff are calling for my punishment. Everyone else is just glad he's gone. Lalonda is mostly silent as her grief collides with her relief in a confusing turmoil of emotions. A town meeting is called in the park so we can use the old bandstand stage and have enough room for everyone. A surprisingly large group gathers to discuss the events of yesterday, and I feel my heart racing a bit more than expected at the prospect of the considerable consequences that could be chosen here.

"She's guilty as the day is long. She should be exiled to the outlands like she deserves!" A deputy speaks up loudly enough to be heard over the crowd.

"You know it's not like that, Ben, now let's just calm down and be civilized for a minute, shall we?" Steven addresses him directly.

Stepping to the very front of the bandstand, Steven hushes the crowd and begins the informal hearing. "Alright, everyone, we do need to hush up and get things started. As the new Sheriff, I intend to ensure that this matter is handled properly."

Steven turns to look at me. "Now, Miss Weber, you have been accused of murder by several of the deputies who served under the Sheriff. Are you prepared to defend yourself?"

"Sheriff, I haven't had time to solicit witnesses, but I believe I have a few people who can speak to the events yesterday."

"Alright then, let's begin. There are several accusers, and I have heard all of them privately. They have decided to elect a single spokesperson. Ben, you want to come up here?" Steven looks to the side where the deputies have congregated.

Ben starts walking purposefully towards the stage.

"Yes, Sir, I surely do! That woman..."

Steven interrupts. "Please be specific, Deputy."

"...Raylene Weber has a history of conflict with the Sheriff. She was even involved in a firefight with several of his men a while back."

Surprised by the incredible exaggerations being given, I can't help but interrupt.

"Sheriff, those of us who were present at that time know that the situation has a lot more to it than is being said. It is a slanderous statement without proper context, and since that situation is not the purpose of today's meeting, it is a bit irrelevant, isn't it?"

"Well... such big fancy words won't get you out of this, tramp! You got history and you can't cover it up anymore!" Ben's aggressive stance and pointed finger stop him a couple of steps away from the center of the stage before he is distracted by Steven.

"Civility and professionalism, Deputy! While I agree that history is important to understanding a situation, Miss Weber is correct that the situation in question is not why we are here. No one was killed, and that altercation ended peacefully *because* of Miss Weber did it, not?"

"Well... " Ben stammers.

"Exactly, so let's move on, please." Steven is embracing his role well and holding the line with more strength than I expected.

"Ok, what about the time he ended up in a physical altercation with her at The Restaurant because she was teasing his... his manliness and then changed her mind?" Ben asks.

"Again, Sheriff, not the whole story, and not relevant." I plead, trying to sound more confident than I am.

"Ben, last warning. Miss Weber, since it is out there, would you like to briefly explain that one as well?" Steven asks.

I sigh. "I'd rather not, but probably should. I was visiting with Lalonda when the Sheriff came into The Restaurant, upset about the situation with the soldiers and how he felt he had been wronged in the way it was handled. He became enraged and violently attacked me in a manner lending to the belief that his intentions were impure, which also left me with several bruises. Bruno and you, Sir, pulled him off of me so I could remove myself from the situation, and he could calm down. There was no teasing involved."

Steven nods and turns back towards Ben. "Ben, do you have factual, relevant information regarding the incident, leaving the Sheriff dead or not?"

"I know the Sheriff was at The Restaurant yesterday, and he was upset with Miss Weber and decided to go have a talk with her about it. The next thing we knew, he was dead at her hand." Ben gestures pointedly at me, his stance growing increasingly aggressive and threatening.

Steven addresses me again. "Miss Weber, do you dispute the fact that you were responsible for the Sheriff's death?"

"Sir, I do take responsibility, but only in part. My actions were those of self-defense."

"Can you walk us through what happened yesterday?" Steven asks.

"Yes, Sir. I was at my home when someone came to the door to warn me that they had overheard the Sheriff's intentions to come to see me, that he was very drunk, angry, and seemed unstable in his thoughts. After the recent incident your deputy mentioned, I did not wish to be caught without a way to defend myself if needed. I sought out my father's shotgun, checked for shells..."

"See? That's premeditation! She wanted to shoot the Sheriff!" Ben shouts, followed by the angry yells of several men behind him.

"ENOUGH! Let her speak." Steven yells back.

"Please continue, Miss Weber."

"Thank you. Before I could even make it to the door, the Sheriff forced his way into my home. He was very agitated and even began breaking things. He advanced towards me as he threatened me, and in fear for my life, I shot him. I immediately began first aid procedures, but the damage was too great.

If I may call a witness, Joshua Pierce came in at that point and can better explain what happened after that."

Steven nods. "That's fine, is Joshua present?"

"Yes, Sir, I am," Joshua calls from the front row of the people standing close to the stage.

"If I may, I heard the shot as I was approaching the house. Running, I came into Ray's living room and saw her kneeling over the Sheriff, applying pressure to his wound, trying to stop the bleeding. Even in his final moments, I saw him raising a gun towards her, which I removed from his hand. The Sheriff's wounds were obviously past repair, and I saw him stop breathing. Ray had gone into shock, so I removed her and made sure she was settled in the next room. Upon returning to the Sheriff moments later, I checked to be sure and found that he had indeed passed. I had word sent to

The Restaurant and to you, Sir, before I did anything else to make sure everything was handled properly. You and your men arrived and managed the scene, then took the Sheriff away. With your permission, I cleaned everything up after you were done, and now here we are."

"Thank you. Miss Weber, do you have any other witnesses you'd like to call?" Steven asks.

"Yes, Sir, I'd like to call Jamal Wilson to speak, please."

"Is Jamal here?"

"Yessir, I's here." Jamal is also at the front of the stage, right next to Joshua.

"Can you give your account of anything said here today?"

"It's like Miss Ray done said. I's at her house gettin' wrapped up as part of my healin', and was 'bout to go home when you came to the door."

"Wait, *you* are the one who warned her? Steven, how could you? Do you not have a single loyal bone in your body? Or maybe this was a plan to knock him off so you could steal his position... You..."

Ben's comment comes as a surprise to everyone, and the crowd becomes a mixture of startled looks and accusing shouts.

Scared, Jamal turns to me. "Miss Ray, did I do wrong?"

I kneel down on the stage to be closer to him.

"No, Jamal, the truth is a good thing, just sometimes better when it is less specific."

Steven, quick to maintain control of the crowd, lest it become a mob, interrupts the shouting crowd. "Hey now, that's enough! Yes, I was the one who told Miss Weber of the Sheriff's intention to visit her and that his state of mind was less than ideal. I swore an oath to protect the citizens of this county, and I take it very seriously, even with the changes that have come to our lives. Wouldn't you have wanted me to do the same had he been coming for you?

At no point did I tell her to kill him, nor did I arm her; I simply gave her warning so she could have a chance to prepare herself. If that is a problem for any of you, we will deal with that later. Right now, we are trying to work out if there should be any further consequences for the death of one of our citizens. Now, hush up!

Jamal, please continue."

"Yessir, so I heard you tellin' Miss Ray that the Sheriff was comin' and in a bad mood 'bout it. I had been at the restaurant workin' at the library earlier, an' he was goin' on about 'er afore I left too. Had been for days, it seemed like. I told 'er so and she sent me home. Said I should tell ever'body to get inside and tell Mama too, so if somethin' happened, hopefully nobody would get caught up in it."

"Or to remove any witnesses," Ben interjects, causing another stir in the crowd.

"Ben, enough. Last warning." Steven is now glaring in Ben's direction, tired of the unnecessary aggravation he is causing the crowd.

"Jamal, did you have anything else to add?" Steven asks.

"Nothin' that ain't been said, Sir, but I do stand with what Miss Ray been sayin' as far as the things I seen."

"Thank you, Jamal. Anyone else, Miss Weber?"

"Sir, Lalonda Pressley has been witness to a lot of these situations, and if she is willing, I'd like to give her the opportunity to speak. If not, I accept that, and I want to respect her time to grieve. Everyone here knows that she and I have not had the most peaceful acquaintance, and given her relationship with the Sheriff, it is likely that she would not be supportive of me in any way."

"You sure you want to call her then?" Steven looks unsure about this choice.

"She deserves the chance to speak if she chooses," I reply quietly.

A voice calls out from way back in the crowd.

"Alright enough. I'll talk, but I don't think any of you will like it."

Lalonda's obviously tear-swollen face and cracking voice betrayed her usually frigid exterior to contain a heart I still hope can be reached one day.

"As much as I can't stand her, what she said is right, but that's not all of it. Brad wanted her, and she turned him down over and over. That and all the stupid insanity of life made him go crazy. He lost himself in it all, and it's all your faults! Instead of helping him, he was put off. Instead of seeing through his meanness, everyone just pushed him away. All your foolishness drove him to drink until he couldn't see what was right in front of him. I'm the only one who cared for him at all, but it wasn't enough…"

Her gentle weeping has returned and is on its way to full-on sobbing. I feel myself wanting to reach out to her so much. It's not possible with the way things are now, but I feel my own eyes beginning to well up again as the power of her sadness reaches my heart.

"Thank you, Lalonda. You have given us all something to think about. Miss Weber, do you have any further witnesses?"

I hang my head just a little, overwhelmed with so many feelings at once. The weight of what is to come is almost more than I can bear.

"No, Sir, anyone else would only be corroborating what has already been said. I would like to ask that in all things, everything I have done, not just this one thing, be accounted for as a consequence and considered."

"Sir, if I may speak once more." Joshua implores.

Steven addresses Joshua, "Mr. Pierce?"

"Sir, I have seen all of the aftermath of this event for Miss Weber, and I have to say that I doubt anything you could do to her would outweigh the pain she is experiencing from having been through all of this. She is already bound by a consequence that will likely never leave her.

In the short time I have known her, she has inspired more people and helped so many to better their lives. She goes out of her way to make things better for complete strangers and sacrifices even more for those she cares for.

I have no doubt that had she had any real choice, the Sheriff would b
standing here with us right now. She is an incredible woman and such
major asset to this and neighboring communities. I hope those things ma
serve to pardon her from further suffering."

"Her suffering? She is still alive at least!" Ben yells out.

Obviously irritated with the continued outbursts, Steven replies. "Ber
you've said your piece. We all understand your feelings and that there ar
several who agree. There are also several here who disagree. We'll have to cal
it to a vote. Everyone who believes Miss Weber should be severely punishec
please move over to my right."

Not surprisingly, a large portion of the deputies moved over quickly, a
well as several people from the south side of town.

"Alright, now y'all realize you could be sentencing her to death, right? l
any of you would like to see a lesser punishment and anyone else who think
something needs to happen, but don't want to see Miss Weber dead o
banished to the outlands, please move to my left."

A fair portion of the crowd began to move that direction, an
thankfully, a few of the braver ones from the first group shifted as well. Th
numbers seemed close between those groups, and it is too hard to tell whic
one is larger.

"Alright, of those who are left, you have two options. If you believe Mi
Weber's statement that her actions were self-defense and that she should b
free to go, please group in the center directly in front of me. For those wh
wish to abstain, please move to the area behind me. Anyone who wishes t
change their votes, please do so now. We will start counting in just
moment."

Joshua is standing in the very center of the front group as close to me a
he can get while still remaining in the crowd to be counted. Standing up o
the stage, I wish he could be here with me, but it looks like I may need ever
vote possible to win this.

"Ok, of those who abstained, I need three volunteers to come count from the stage."

Time feels slow to move, and things begin to sound far away again. How long has it been since I took a breath? I open my eyes to see Joshua and the ceiling of the stage area.

"What happened?" I ask.

"You passed out. I don't think you were breathing while they were counting. Does anything hurt?" He asks, worry flooding his face.

"I'm not sure. I'd say my pride, but I'm not sure how much of that I have left." I try to chuckle, but fail.

"Ok, well, let's get you up then. They have finished counting."

"Oh, Joshua, I'm afraid." I clutch onto the arm of his shirt as he helps me to stand. He puts his arm around me, both in comfort and stability.

"It'll be alright, I'm right here."

Chapter Twenty-Three

Choice and Consequence

The counts are all in and have been confirmed. Those who want the most severe punishment total 28. Those who believe there should be a lesser punishment total 36. Those who think there should be no further punishment...”

Joshua's arm is around me, pulling me even closer to him. I can't help but wonder whether this is because he is trying to support my emotions or just be prepared for another fainting spell.

“...total 42.”

I had forgotten to breathe again, but this number and the realization that I was free to go back to... well, things will never be the same, but at least I can still be free to help people, raise Matthew, and not be exiled or dead.

Ben steps forward and begins pointing at the other groups.

“You people realize you are freeing a murderer back amongst you, right? Unbelievable!”

Several nods and murmurs of agreement came from the right.

Steven moves over closer to that side, and the crowd wishing for severe punishment. "Ben, please meet me afterward. The vote was fair, and I expect that this will be the end of this terrible business. As everyone is aware, I am now the Sheriff, and I was the next with seniority in the department. I would like you all to know that I intend to uphold the law to the best of my ability, regardless of who may be causing the trouble. There are too few of us left, and there is so much that needs to be done for us to all make it through. We need to come together as a community, and I hope that this difficult time may serve to bring about that change instead of dividing us. Thank you all for coming and participating in this." Steven pauses to look at me.

"Miss Weber, you are free to go."

"Thank you, Stev... Sheriff."

"Come on, let's get you out of here." Joshua takes my hand and starts to draw me away through the center crowd, thankfully mostly made up of friendly faces. The number of people trying to speak to me as we pass is overwhelming. Most want to either congratulate or offer some sort of empathetic acknowledgment, but then there are the faces moving closer who will not be getting their wish. Not today, at least. So much pain and now so much hate just pierce through me like a hot knife. Will things ever be peaceful?

"Yes, please. I would like to go home, not the one in town, though."

We have finally made it through the majority of the crowd. Joshua stops and turns to face me again.

"The farm you mean?"

My hand drops.

"Yes, I need to get away for a while. I think I'll take Matthew out there. It's been a while since he's seen the place. I have no business to ask, but if you would like to come as well, you would be welcome. It would be nice to have someone around for a while if you have the time."

Joshua's concern melts into kindness. "I would like that very much."

I try to smile just a little. "Ok, it'll take me a bit to pack and such, do you need to go home first?"

"No, I have things down here. I always come prepared in case I can't make it back up for a few days."

I nod. "Smart! Ok, well, I will see you at my house in a bit then."

Joshua gently squeezes my arm.

"Sounds perfect. Hey, you did well today."

"I'm just thankful I had people here to help. I'm not sure how much more I can take after all this." Tears are threatening my cheeks once more.

"Well, hopefully this will be a nice break. Lord knows you deserve it!"

"Thanks, Joshua."

Walking back to the house, I can't help but stop and stare at the bare floor where the rug once was, the rug and so much more. Fighting to break the trance threatening to take me over, I find myself walking down the hall to pack things for both Matty and me. I have most of the things we will need loaded when Lola brings Matty back to the house.

"He wanted to see you, an' make sure you was doin' ok."

I hug Matthew tightly. "Thanks, Lola."

"You goin' somewhere?" Lola asks.

Bending slightly with my hands on my knees, I address Matty, "Matthew, do you want to go out to the farm for a few days?"

He looks slightly confused.

"Sure, but why? Aren't all the animals gone?"

"They are, but several of them are next door at another farm, so we can go visit them. There is a pond out in one of the fields with plenty of fish, and no one has been catching them. Would you like to have a fish fry?" I ask, trying to sound happy and excited, instead of full of pain.

Matthew makes that easier without even realizing it. His excitement is effortlessly contagious.

"Oh yes! I love fish! Can I fish for them?"

"Absolutely! I have another surprise too. You know Mr. Joshua, who has come by a few times?" I ask.

Matty nods quickly. "Yes, he's nice. He knows a lot about the plants and animals outside."

"Yes, he does."

How I needed the positive feelings coming from this sweet boy. Even with the weight I've felt, his excitement brings a smile to my face. It's amazing how much physically smiling can bring just a little light back to your soul.

"He is actually going to come with us. I told him about the farm, and he wanted to come visit it also. What do you think of that?"

Matthew taps his chin thoughtfully. "Is he going to fish too?"

"He most likely will."

The smile on Matthew's face couldn't be bigger. "Cool! We'll be sure to catch a lot if he helps!"

"I'm sure he'll be a great help. Let's go get the rest of the things we will need packed so we can head out soon." I stand back up and gently push Matty's shoulder in the direction of his room.

A few minutes later, there is a quick knock and the front door opens to reveal Joshua already back. "You guys ready to go? We can take my truck if you like."

I shake my head. "I'd like to take mine if that's ok. You can drive, though. She hasn't seen the farm in months, and it just seems right. Plus, I've already been loading our gear in the back."

"Sounds good, I'll toss mine in also." He starts to go back out, but I turn to stop him before he goes outside.

"I need to talk to one of the neighbors for a bit. With us leaving town, someone will need to manage a few things."

"Do whatever you need to. I'll hang out with Matty until you come back." Joshua offers a reassuring smile. I needed it.

Walking up to Mama Lou's house, I know she is the only person who can organize this. She answers the door and wraps me in one of her amazing hugs before I can even get a word out.

"Oh sweet girl, I's so sorry for all you goin' through, but that man was evil, an' the world is better for 'is leavin' it."

It takes a moment to find my voice through the tightness that has overtaken my throat, wrapped up in the arms of another safe place.

"Thank you, Mama Lou." Whispering is about all I can manage right now.

She finally lets me go and gently holds my arms... a nice change from the way they've been treated lately.

"What can I do to help?"

"Mama, I was hoping I could ask you a really big favor. I need to take some time away, so I'm taking Matty to the farm for a few days. The only problem is that there are a couple of things in the works that need some supervision. The first is the deal with the other towns for the windmills. Last time, a side deal was proposed by Andy in Carlsburg, and a trailer was dropped off in the scrap yard as part of the new deal, but Marshall in Harrison wasn't feeling good about it. So when the parts for the next batch of windmills are picked up from the scrap yard, Marshall needs to have either accepted the deal so he can keep the trailer and provide the parts, or the trailer will need to be brought back to Andy.

The second thing is the work on the high school for the homeless kids. I have a few people starting to work on it, but the leaders of that group are having a hard time trusting that they will be respected as equals. We need to make sure that the work continues and that they are given that respect. Otherwise, it could all fall apart. This all needs to keep going with or without me, and I think you may well be the best person I can trust to do it right."

"I'm honored you think so high of me." Mama Lou replies with a sweet face and a gentle smile.

I attempt a smile, but it doesn't come. I'm so emotionally overwhelmed and exhausted, it's all I can do to hold it together and handle the absolutely necessary things.

"I really do. If you want to involve a couple of the neighbors like Jed and Brian, please do. I trust you all completely, and I feel terrible for asking so much of you. Feel free to harvest what you can from the garden and share with anyone else who helps as well." A couple of tears threaten to fall, with the weight of so many needs piled up, and so much to ask for.

"Askin' so much of us? Listen 'ere girl, you do and do and do so much for alla us, if we can't pitch in for a few days, then we don' have no business calling ourselves friends." Mama Lou wraps me back up in that amazing hug of hers.

A few tears fall, and I sniffle, no longer able to restrain them in the embrace of such kindness. "Thank you so much, Mama Lou. I am planning on being back in a few days. I just really want to give everything a chance to calm down and to get a little peace back myself. I think I've needed a break for a while, really, so a few quiet days on the farm and I should be back to full strength."

"You do what you need to. We'll be 'ere when you get back."

*****

Driving out to the farm was both beautiful and strange. I didn't realize just how much I missed the country. The sweet smell of hay and grass, the open views of the fields with lines of trees along the edges. The air feels cleaner, fresher, and the sky seems so much bigger. Watching the simplicity of animals out grazing without any of the cares of those responsible for them, they just spend their days being themselves.

The roads are completely empty, and where there used to be tractors running, the fields are either wild and overrun by plants they've chosen for themselves or have been partially managed using a horse and plow like they would have been so long ago.

The route to the farm is mindlessly familiar, but I haven't had to give directions before. We almost miss a turn as I lose myself to it all. My eyes close as my hand goes out the window into the breeze of air flowing past. As children, Cameron and I used to play hand planes in the air out the window by closing our fingers together and letting the air move our hands in all directions as if we were pilots flying freely without a care.

"Oh shoot, turn here!" I quickly point across to the left, where the road is coming up fast. Joshua quickly slows the truck just in time to make the turn onto what is left of the familiar old dirt road.

"Good thing I was taking it easy on your old truck here." His joking comment makes us both smile.

"I'm sorry, I was a little too far into my thoughts, I think."

"I saw that and I'm glad you came back before we ended up in the capital!" Joshua winks, adding charm to his teasing.

The light banter is fun and serves to add to the pleasant feelings I've lost myself to.

Just a few moments and a couple turns later, I can see the barn and house rising up in the distance. My breath catches when I see the state it's in. Pulling into the driveway, it is obvious that someone has ransacked the place. *The guns!*

Jumping from the truck the second it stops, I race out to the barn and begin throwing things frantically, trying to uncover the floorboards hiding my secrets. Joshua comes in just as I uncover them to find that they may be the only things that have not been disturbed. Sliding to the floor with my face in my hands takes all the willpower I have to try not to cry. *Why did this happen? Why couldn't we just have a nice break from all of the awful things in the world?*

"Are you ok?"

I can't help but jump, having not heard Joshua come in.

"You scared me!" I half cry.

Joshua kneels down on the floor next to me.

"I'm sorry, I thought you heard me come in. I left Matthew in the truck for now and checked to be sure there wasn't anyone still around. What can I do for you?"

"*Do?* What can anyone do? People are just awful!"

The tears are coming freely now. The hurt and anger, combined with all of the intense emotions of late, just won't stay inside anymore. Joshua moves to sit on the floor to put his arm around me once more. My clenched fists won't release, and even with his comforting embrace, there is still too much emotion to be settled quickly.

"Auntie Ray?" A small voice calls out from the main barn door.

"We're in here, Matthew, she's ok," Joshua calls back.

Matthew strolls back into the doorway of this little side room we are in.

"Auntie, what happened to the farm?"

It is so hard to pretend you aren't upset and get away with it around most kids anyway, but Matthew was gifted with an extra dose of empathy, and I know he already feels my turmoil. His sweet voice, filled with concern more appropriate of a much older child, reveals just that.

"Oh sweetie, someone chose to come looking for things that didn't belong to them, and instead of being respectful about it, like we are in town, they didn't take care with their search and left us quite a big mess, didn't they?"

"Yeah... Do we have to clean it up now?" Again, with maturity far past his years, he already knows the answer.

I wipe the tears from my face, fighting for control over my emotions and the strength needed for the task at hand. "Well, we'll probably have to clean up a few things in the house for sure. I promise we are still going to do some fishing and exploring like we wanted to, though."

Matthew's smile comes so easily, and his willingness to help, even in the face of such a tremendous job, reveals such strength of character. "Ok, I'd like that. I don't mind helping to clean either. Grandma always had me help Grandpa with chores when I came out anyway. I'd like to do some for them now."

"You are such an amazing boy, Matthew. Come here, huh?" Joshua makes room, and Matthew comes to sit on my lap. Hugging this sweet boy and thinking of my parents and all of the work they did on this farm starts the tears again. This time they are not nearly so hot as before, and I feel just a bit of that rage disappear.

Heading back to the house after concealing my stash safely below the floorboards again, I try to brace myself for the inevitable disaster inside. The kitchen door is open and, by the looks of things, has been for a while. Cabinets and drawers are still open, a chair is on its side by the table, and broken ceramic pieces crunch on the floor as we step inside.

Looking down, it's the mug that my daddy used for his coffee every morning. Suddenly, the need to make things right brings out the stubborn determination I get from my mama and fills me with a resolve I didn't expect.

"Matthew, do you remember where Grandma kept the broom and dustpan? Can you please go get those and any other cleaning supplies you see? Joshua, would you mind bringing the truck to park behind the house? I'm not sure I want to announce our presence any more than we already have. If you don't mind unloading, there is a door back there that I will unlock if it isn't already. Everything can just come in wherever you can find a spot."

"Sure thing."

The next hour passes quickly as the kitchen is put to rights, as much as possible anyway, as are the living room, and my brother's old bedroom for Matthew.

"Auntie, can we stop chores for a bit? I'm getting pretty hungry."

Looking up from the papers I'm straightening, I can see through the window that the light is moving well into the evening.

"I'm so sorry, guys, I think I lost track of time. How do tomato sandwiches sound?"

Joshua stands up from his spot on the floor, gathering up more of the mess. "I'd eat just about anything, I think. Do you need a hand?"

"No, thank you, I think I'd like to do this myself. Mama almost never let anyone lift a finger in the kitchen who had been working. I don't think she'd like it if I broke that tradition."

The sandwiches are easy enough to put together. The fresh bread was made by a neighbor down the street in town, and the tomatoes came from our backyard garden. I had just a tiny bit of cheese left from a recent trip out to the farms to trade that barely made an appearance on the four sandwiches cut diagonally into eight triangles. A few apples cored and sliced as companions would have to do. Hopefully, we can get some fishing in tomorrow for some good protein.

"This is really good, Ray, thank you." Joshua's genuine smile accentuates his gratitude.

"Yeah, Auntie, you know I love tomato san'wiches, 'speshly with cheese!" Matthew's happy grin never ceases to amaze me. He is so pleased with simple things. It's a blessing these days, to be sure.

"Thanks, guys, and thank you for working so hard. Your daddy would be proud of the job you did in his old room. I'm not sure he even kept it that clean!" I say, smiling at Matthew.

"You think so? I'd like him to be proud of me." Matthew asks, thoughtfully.

Joshua chimes in before I have a chance.

"I'm sure he is, buddy, daddies tend to be proud of their sons from the get-go, and you are such a great kid, there is no doubt that you give him good reason."

"Thanks, Mr. Joshua."

I take a moment to appreciate the sweet relationship that is building between these two.

"Alright, mister, time to head to bed, we have a big day of fishing ahead of us tomorrow!"

Even though I know we have cleared the house and been in it for hours, I can't shake the uneasy feeling that we aren't alone. The doors are locked, something practically unheard of in this house while I was growing up. *I better walk Matthew to bed just in case.* Thankfully, the room is empty, and Matthew settles in easily.

"I like being here again. I miss grandma and grandpa sometimes, and I miss daddy all the time. It feels good to be around where they were."

I sit next to Matthew on the bed with my arm around him.

"Oh buddy, I miss them too. I understand what you're feeling. It's nice to be here. It almost feels like they are still around, doesn't it?"

"Yeah." Matthew looks up at me. "I know they aren't, but I like to think maybe they are sometimes."

I rub his arm gently. "Well, as long as we remember them, they are never all the way gone from here, and someday we'll get to see them again."

Matthew leans his head into my shoulder. "I love you, auntie."

I lean my head on top of his. "I love you, too, Matty." Standing up, I pull up his covers and kiss him on the forehead.

"I love you. Sleep well and I'll see you in the morning."

Chapter Twenty-Four

Past and Future

"Some day, huh?" Joshua asks from his spot on the couch as I walk back into the living room.

"That's an understatement." I wrap my arms around myself, rubbing my hands over them as if I'm cold.

"I never expected things to be like this. It has me pretty creeped out, honestly, and I keep feeling like someone else is here watching somehow. That probably sounds crazy, right?" I ask, feeling unsure.

"No, you don't sound crazy. Stressed, maybe, and understandably so given the state of the place, but not crazy."

I start to head to the kitchen to clean up and finish putting things right in there. To my surprise, everything has already been cleaned up. I turn back towards Joshua.

"Oh, thank you for clearing the table and cleaning up. I should probably get to work on a couple more bedrooms."

"Why don't you sit down here with me instead?" Joshua motions to the empty seat next to him.

"Well... but..." I look around at all the work still needing to be done and try to protest, but the long hours and emotional exhaustion are making a rest sound really good.

Seeing my conflict, Joshua beckons further. "You need to relax for a bit. Besides, I'd like to hear more about this place."

"Alright, just for a bit though."

Joshua is sitting on the sofa that Mama always wanted to refinish. It's blue and cream checked pattern with little Texas stars in the squares looked more like a tablecloth than a piece of furniture, but it was comfortable and left to us when Grandma died, which made it just a little more special. I expected it would be mine whenever I moved out, I guess it is now.

I choose to join him on the couch instead of either of the other two chairs in the living room. They had always been reserved for each of my parents before, and it just didn't seem right to change that now. Turning our bodies so that we face each other comfortably, we aren't touching, but are close enough that it wouldn't be hard to change.

"So, what would you like to know?" I ask.

Joshua smiles. "Anything you want to tell me. I want to know more about this force of nature I've come to the country with. What is the first thing you think about?"

"Ha! Force of nature, huh? Well, let's see... I told you that I grew up here. My older brother Cameron is Matthew's father and my only sibling. We own about 320 acres total between farm fields and pastures, which is about average for the farms around here. It's nice because no one has a giant industrial operation, so you still get to know your neighbors, and people still help each other out.

When Daddy was in his prime, he managed to do almost everything by himself. He'd hire on one or two hands to help with a big project like harvest, but otherwise, it was just us.

I think you would've liked my daddy. He was a huge bear of a man with an even bigger heart. He was well-read, although you wouldn't believe it at first glance. Most of the library books you saw were originally his, and he had read every one at least once. When I was little, and on to when I was probably much too old for such things, he used to pick one of the books to read to me at night. As I got older, I would take turns with him. It was a sweet time, just the two of us together. It may be one of the things I miss the most." It's hard not to be saddened by these thoughts, but I try to focus on the words and not so much on the feelings.

Mama was a beauty, but she could hold her own, too. She was always so strong, stubborn... determined in everything."

"Hmm, all of that sounds familiar."

There goes that wink again, and my cheeks!

"Oh, whatever! When she and Daddy were just getting to know each other, apparently, one of the boys said something about how girls, specifically Mama, couldn't keep up with them around the farm, which was a big mistake. They challenged her to a race, doing a bunch of things in a barn, and chose Daddy to go against her as the champion for the boys. She beat him with so much time to spare, she went inside and fixed herself a glass of sweet tea. By the time the boys came back up to the house, she was cleaned up and sitting on the porch with her tea and a book. Daddy always said that was the moment he knew she was the one."

"Sounds like the women in your family have a tradition of being impressive." Joshua's grin is a perfect match to his semi-teasing tone.

"She did for sure. Anyway, I grew up helping out around here. I was a 4-H member as soon as I turned five and kept at it until I was 18. So between the farm, school, church, 4-H, and then later managing the store, I never went to college. I expected I might when this or that happened, but then excuses kept piling up.

I did apprentice for a while under the holistic veterinarian who lived up the road a ways. That's where I learned a lot of what I know about healing. In reality, I just don't think I figured out what I wanted to be when I grew up. I still don't think I really know."

"I'm pretty sure you're doing what you are meant to do, even if it wasn't what you expected, and you already had the perfect education for it." No more teasing, just kindness this time.

"Perhaps. I hope so anyway. There is so much wrong these days. I wish I understood all of this craziness. I mean, why attack and take us back to basically the dark ages, then just disappear again? It just doesn't make sense, you know?" I look Joshua in the eyes, almost as if I want him to have the answers to these questions. I know he doesn't, but he seems to have so many others.

Joshua half-shrugs, "I have wondered about that myself. Things like where did everyone go, and what is out past the boundary that we aren't allowed to see?"

"Right! I have heard of people trying to find out and never coming back. I suppose that makes sense, but I guess I just can't make sense of the rest of it. I've thought about trying to see what is over there myself, but I have Matthew." I glance in the direction of the hall at the thought.

Joshua looks at me with disbelief and emphatically replies, "You are much too important to the community, too! I mean, would even half of the improvements have been made without you? People would probably be starving and not nearly so civil without your help."

"Well, thank you for the confidence. I don't think I could ask anyone else to do it, though. What if they also didn't come back? I can't be responsible for anyone else dying or getting hurt." I shake my head and look down carrying the weight of such a thought.

"I'm sure they would only be able to go if you were sure they understood the risks," Joshua says gently.

I nod. "Probably. The thought does come up from time to time anyway."

"Maybe it is something that can be explored more now that you have those tanks and such, although they would make the element of surprise pretty much useless." Joshua chuckles.

"Oh yeah! If anything, I would probably try for a completely clandestine, almost guerrilla-style trip. Stick to the shadows, silent, and as little trace as possible. I wish Cameron was here to help with something like that. He used to sneak up on me even as kids, and I would never know where he was until he was literally right on top of me. Add in his military training, and honestly, I can't believe he was among the disappeared. I thought for sure he would evade whatever it was that happened to them."

Concern furrows Joshua's brow. "Is there any chance he did and just hasn't been able to make it back?"

I shake my head. "I doubt it, I saw him that morning and he was headed down to post just south of town. I don't see anything keeping him from Matthew if nothing else."

"I'm sorry, Ray." Empathetic sadness takes a turn. The genuine nature that makes up this man is ever endearing.

"It's ok. It does make me sad to think about it all, but the truth is, as much as I miss him, I'm glad to have had him as a brother. He was a good man." I sigh, then switch the subject away from myself.

"So, enough about me, what's your origin story?"

The shifting in his seat betrays his discomfort at the quick segue. "Oh well, you already know most of it. I grew up on the mountain, but never really fit in. I wasn't ever satisfied with the way things were. My mother was stubborn as well, but she was also understanding. It was a great combination in that she fought to protect my educational pursuits when many of the elders thought I was weird or doing something I shouldn't be, just because she saw that it was so important to me. You may have seen her in town before. She used to come down with preserves, pies, and fruit to sell. She is actually the one who planted the apple orchard."

I pause in thought.

"Actually, I think I do remember seeing her. Did she have long, dark brown hair, bright blue eyes, a sturdy but slender frame, and always in a dress?" I ask, thoughtfully.

Joshua pauses, surprised by my answer. "That's actually a perfect description of her. She was down there making money so I would be able to go to school. I was only able to finish my associate's degree with the money she earned for all of those years.

I was also working and would have been able to afford my Bachelors, but then she fell ill and I came home to try to help out. She passed away a few months later, and I never left again after that." Joshua is looking down at his hands now, clasped in front of him as he leans forward onto his knees.

"Oh, Joshua, I'm so sorry." I reach out to touch his shoulder. He looks back up at me and offers a small smile.

"Don't be. My mother was an amazing woman, and she left this earth the better for her having been in it. I do miss her, but I'm glad I came home to be with her. I don't think I could have lived with myself if I hadn't." Joshua leans back into the couch, resting his arm on the back toward me, and bringing his foot up onto his knee.

"Besides, I'm about as happy as I think I could be with my life as it is now. I mean, I'm healthy, I have plenty to keep me that way, and I have met this wonderful, beautiful woman who surprises me at every turn. What more could a guy ask for?"

If my face had been near a fireplace, I could have lit the fire for how warm my cheeks were that moment.

I barely stammer a response. "I... I don't know what to say. I mean I..."

"Ray, you don't have to say anything. I only hope that maybe we can use the time we spend out here to just see what this could be. Since the first time we met, I find myself more and more drawn to you. You are smart, funny, and you care so deeply for everyone you meet. I try, but often find that I can't get you out of my head, and you fit so well there. I'm sorry if I've been too forward; if I have learned anything, it is that there just isn't time to leave things unsaid. This new world we live in is too unsteady for that. I don't want to put any pressure on you at all; I don't have any untoward expectations..."

His hand found mine as our eyes meet.

"I just want to be near you."

Those eyes, the same brilliant blue as his mother's, are pulling me in, and I feel myself entranced in the way they seem to look right through me. His words and all of the thoughts and feelings I've been storing away about him suddenly appear from the corners of my mind where they were hiding. I think I may want to give it all a chance. How often does love come around in a post-apocalyptic, crazy world like this?

My mind is spinning, and the room seems to be all but gone as we're safely sealed into this bubble of our own creation. I feel him moving closer like he feels this too. The arms that have comforted me so many times now feel different. Instead of comfort, they have a longing in them, a need my own arms share as we move closer together...

"Hey, Ray, what's up?"

The trance is strong and slow to break. I slowly turn to look toward the voice in the doorway...

"Cameron?"

...to be continued.